CAPTAIN COMBAT:
LOW CEILING FOR NAZI HELL HAWKS

LOW CEILING FOR
NAZI HELL HAWKS

By Barry Barton

STEEGER BOOKS • 2021

CHAPTER 1
THE DEAD STAY DEAD

S LIDING HIS empty glass along the top of the bar to the mess corporal for a refill, Captain Bill Combat, American-born ace of the British Royal Air Force, turned slightly and scowled out the mess window. The fog that had been there since dawn was still hanging low over the English south coast drome of the 42nd Home Defense Squadron. However, as Combat peered at the soup, it seemed to be thinning out and rising slightly.

"Not thinking of going up in that stuff, are you, Captain?" the mess corporal asked, giving Combat a fresh drink. "It's real bird-walking weather, this is."

"Three solid days of it," the Yank grunted. "I think I'll give it a try, though. My ship needs testing. And besides, if I sit around here doing nothing much longer I'll go plain nuts."

"It's going to be a blinking long war, sir," the corporal said meaningly. "No sense taking chances, I say."

Combat grinned and drained his drink.

"Maybe you've got something there, Corporal," he said. "I'll remember that bit of advice. If the Colonel comes looking for me, tell him I'm upstairs... I hope."

The mess corporal agreed and let it go at that without further argument. He knew it would be futile. When that "wild-crazy

Low Ceiling for Nazi Hell Hawks

by BARRY BARTON

Yank" made up his mind to do something, all the King's horses and all the King's men couldn't stop him.

As a matter of fact, something more than the mere desire to fly sent Combat out the mess door and over to the row of hangars. He couldn't have put it into words. It was, perhaps, the combination of a hunch, a strange feeling of foreboding, and the nervous urge to see what was beyond the fog—even if it was only the blue sky. In short, Combat had the strange sensation—which comes to fighting men—that something was about to happen. Perhaps he was crazy, but it had always been a policy of his to follow a hunch right through to the end, and he had no thought of making an exception this time.

And so he ordered his trim, speedy Hawker Hurricane out of B Flight hangar, and chose to ignore the blank amazement on the face of the Flight Sergeant. Ten minutes later he went roaring out across the field, leaving a collection of slowly shaking heads behind him. The instant he was clear he cranked up the wheels, flew straight for a couple of hundred yards, then hauled the nose up into the fog. At six thousand feet he pushed up into a five hundred foot channel of clear air between the fog layers. He leveled off and flew southward down the channel, then started to nose up through to the top of the upper layer… but he didn't.

He didn't because at that moment his steel grey eyes suddenly caught a glimpse of the plane. At first it was no more than a smudgy dot far off his right wing. He veered that way, opened up his throttle a bit more and went thundering toward it. A moment later he caught a clear silhouette of the plane against a thin patch of the fog the sun was trying to break through. One good look brought him up straight in the seat.

"What the hell?" he muttered aloud. "That job's a British sport cabin ship, or else I'm the King of Siam. And what's a sport job doing—flying around in this stuff?"

He fed more hop to the many horses in the Hurricane's nose and started after the mystery ship in earnest. Perhaps its pilot saw him coming and wanted no part of him, or perhaps the pilot would have changed his course at that moment, anyway. At any rate, the small ship suddenly swung around toward the east and started up into the second layer of the dense, heavy fog.

COMBAT INSTANTLY pulled his own nose up, and in practically nothing flat his speedy ship had climbed right through into clear air and sunshine. It was when he ripped up through into the sunshine that he got proof of what he'd suspected for the last few minutes. It was that the fog was only local. It ended exactly on the shore of the Channel, some four miles dead ahead of him. It was as though the stuff had been cut through with a huge knife, the half that hung over the Channel blown away, and the other half anchored fast to England's shores.

Throttling, Combat loafed along the top of the fog waiting for the sport ship to break out into the clear. For the next five or ten minutes there was no sign of the other crate, and little fears began to snap at Combat. Had the other pilot seen him and doubled back in the fog to get free of him? Somehow that seemed unlikely, because after all, both were British ships, and although there were damn few sport planes being flown over England these days, sight of them in the air was not unusual to R.A.F. pilots on patrol.

"Yet this is no weather for a crate like that to be up," Combat told himself as he searched the surrounding sky and the crest of the fog bank. "And come to think of it, I don't know of any field...."

The rest stopped dead on his tongue. At that moment the sport cabin popped up through the fog less than a quarter of a mile away. In a flash Combat kicked rudder and belted the throttle and swung toward it. He could see two men in the cabin, but before he could get a good look at them the little craft seemed to fall off on one wing and go plopping down out of sight into the fog. But like a cork in the trough of a heavy sea, it came popping right up into view again. And it was then Combat saw that the two men in the cabin were at death grips with each other.

Sliding in as close as he dared, the Yank let fly with a short burst of Vickers bullets across the top wing of the smaller ship to attract the attention of those inside. However, he might just as well have drilled his shots right straight into the cabin for all the attention they got him. The ship was flying itself, while the pilot and passenger grappled with each other, one minute in clear view to Combat, and the next down out of sight on the cabin floor.

Then suddenly one of the fighting men broke loose. He lunged for the small cabin door and slammed it open in spite of the prop-wash whipped back by the propeller. Helpless to do anything about it, Combat watched the man dive out into thin air. Too soon the man yanked the rip-cord ring of the seat-pack 'chute he wore. Impulsively Combat bellowed a cry of warning, but it was too late. The prop-wash caught the small pilot 'chute the instant it hit the air and whirled it back against the tail section of the ship. There it fouled, and as the dangling man tried frantically to jerk and pull himself free, the main envelope of 'chute silk was whipped back and slashed to ribbons on the tail of the plane. The shroud lines snapped and the dangling man dropped earthward like a lump of lead as the small plane went careening crazily off to the left.

During the strange fight inside the small cabin plane, the ship had drifted far to the southwest and well clear of the bank of fog. Impulsively Combat took his eyes off the careening plane and watched the dot that was a human being go hurtling earthward, with strips of torn parachute silk flapping out behind. In the last couple of hundred feet Combat lost him against the dark ground. An instant later, though, a great sheet of red flame and swirling black smoke spewed up from the ground. For a second Combat stared unbelieving down at that splash of hell's inferno.

"Good God, a human bomb?" he choked out. "But that's impossible! He wasn't carrying anything in his hands. He…."

The Yank cut off the rest and snapped his eyes back at the careening sports plane as a sudden thought came to him. Had that small ship dropped a bomb, and had that been the explosion he had seen below? He peered hard at the flip-flopping ship for an answer, but there was no bomb-rack slung under the fuse-lage between the landing gear wheels. And it certainly seemed unlikely that the one left in the plane had tossed anything out by hand. The man was now fighting for his own life—fighting to regain control of the little plane and head it earthward. As Combat watched the man he saw him slump over in the seat three times, then desperately struggle up straight again.

"That lad's pretty far gone," Combat heard his own lips mutter. "Ten to one he won't make it, but I sure hope he does. What's happened doesn't make sense."

HAULING HIS own throttle all the way back, Combat

followed the other ship down inch by inch. When the small job was still some six hundred feet or so off the ground, its pilot tried to veer it around and down to a fairly smooth patch of meadow. However, he appeared not to have strength enough left in his battered body. The small ship turned a hair or two toward the smooth patch, but that was as far as it went. For the fourth and last time the pilot in the pit slumped over to the side, and this time he wasn't able to pull himself up straight again. The little cabin plane, its engine now dead, nosed over and down toward the earth.

By the grace of God and pilots' luck, the ship smacked against a tree top. The mess of branches acted as a life net for only a minute. They snapped back and virtually flung the small plane down onto the ground, and it struck hard and crumpled up like so much colored tinfoil. Hardly had the plane crashed than Combat had whipped his pursuit ship down to a fast landing in a field some seventy yards away. The instant he could wheel-brake to a stop, he slammed back the cockpit's glass cowling, leaped out, and went pounding over to the wreck.

And he was not a second too soon. The crash had split open a feed line, and the raw gas spilling down onto the hot engine had burst into flame. Through the cloud of black smoke that swirled upward, Combat saw the huddled form of the pilot. By a miracle of miracles he was still alive and striving weakly to pull himself clear of the flames.

"Coming, buddy!" Combat shouted, and then filled his lungs with air.

Keeping his head low and holding his breath, he plunged into the blazing ship, ripping and yanking broken spars and struts away with his bare hands. Then, when it seemed as though his lungs were going to explode in his chest, he managed to get his hands on the struggling man. A thousand years later Combat had dragged him free and well clear of the ship. And no sooner had he stumbled to the ground with the man than the flames reached the small and still undamaged emergency gas tank and it let go with a roar.

Shielding the half unconscious man with his own body, Combat waited until the shower of burning embers had dropped safely back to earth. Then he pushed up on his knees and stared down into the pain-whitened face. The man's eyes opened and stared up glassily into his.

"Who are you?" Combat asked him. "Who was the other lad with you? What happened?"

The glassy eyes remained fixed on Combat, and the man's lips didn't move. The Yank was about to repeat his questions when the other's lips did part and a jumble of sounds came from between them. The man was speaking German.

"Number Thirty-Six... swine dog... tell Number Thirty-Six... *Der Fuehrer*... it is all settled... all is ready... the *schweinehund*... he thought he was clever, *ja?*... Well... he...."

The disconnected jumble of German trailed off into silence. Stunned for the moment by the sound of German spoken there on English soil, Combat could only stare wide-eyed down at the man. Suddenly a startled light leaped into the other's eyes and changed swiftly to one of stark hatred. Froth sprayed from his lips as he choked out the words, *"Leiber Gott,* you are not…! You are swine English!"

Pain creased the man's face as he suddenly lurched to one side and flashed a hand downward. In that same second, however, Combat hurled his own body to one side. The Luger, clutched in the bleeding fingers of the crash victim, spat flame and sound, and an invisible messenger of death ripped through the radio phone flap of Combat's helmet and zinged off into space.

"Hey, what the hell?" the Yank bellowed, and lunged for the Luger.

He got possession of the gun in nothing flat, but he did not get an answer to his question. The man was dead.

CHAPTER 2
DER TAG

HERMANN PEIPLOW, chief of Nazi Intelligence, sat in his steel walled office across the street from the Chancellery in Berlin, drumming his thick fingers on the top of his huge desk and staring flint-eyed at the short-wave radio panel fitted to the opposite wall. The blinking of a small green light on the desk pulled his eyes off the wall, and he jabbed one of a row of buttons along the edge of the desk and turned his gaze toward the steel door of the room. It swung open with a soft clicking sound and two men entered the room. One was Franz Khole, of the blood-letting Nazi secret police, the Gestapo. The other was the all-powerful commander of the state, *Herr* Gruber, a middle-aged man with mustache and a small Van

Dyke beard.—*Der Fuehrer.*

Gruber ignored Peiplow's flourishing salute. He snapped his eyes toward the radio panel, then snapped them back to Peiplow. "You have received no word, *Herr* Peiplow? What has happened?"

"I do not know, yet, *Fuehrer,*" the chief of Intelligence replied. Then as his cobra black eyes glittered, "But somebody shall pay for it, when I do. *Lieber Gott*, yes!"

Gruber snorted and made an impatient gesture with his hands.

"Why don't you know?" he demanded. "Can you not contact any one of your agents in any part of the world from this room? Did you not ask me to come here to hear the complete test reports from London? *Herr* Peiplow, I am not pleased with you. Nobody in all the Reich keeps me waiting."

"And they shall pay for doing so, my *Fuehrer,*" Peiplow said in a humble voice. "But we must wait. For two hours, now, I have kept the wave-length to London open, but no word comes through. Something very serious has happened."

"What about Number Thirty-Six?" Gruber demanded. "You have made contact with him?"

"A message has been sent to him," the chief of Intelligence nodded. "He will meet you in Zone K as you have ordered. But the meeting will be of no importance until we receive a complete report from England. *Gott*, it is most trying on one's nerves."

As Peiplow spoke the last he gave the radio panel a savage, venomous glare that should have melted all the tube filaments right then and there. A moment later, though, he forgot all about the silent secret wave length radio in his surprise at the green light flashing on his desk. He stared at it, scowled, then stretched out his hand and poked one of the buttons. The heavy steel door opened instantly and two men stepped through.

One was in the uniform of an English flying officer. The other was dressed in London's best Bond Street attire, but despite the snappy Nazi salute he gave, his slightly moon-shaped face was a picture of complete misery and dejection.

Gruber, Khole, and Peiplow stared open-mouthed at the two arrivals, and then the *Fuehrer* found his tongue.

"You, Thirty-Six?" he barked and pointed a picture at the pilot. "What are you doing here in Germany? *Mein Gott*, have you gone mad?"

"It was an emergency, *Fuehrer*," the pilot said, and nodded his head toward his companion. "He left an SOS note at my London place, and I contacted him as soon as I could. He… Perhaps he had better fell you his story, *Fuehrer*."

All eyes became focused on the civilian. The man cringed and swallowed repeatedly.

"Well?" Peiplow suddenly boomed, shattering the silence. "What has the second in charge of the London area got to say? Where is von Berne? Did he send you to report in person?"

The civilian gulped, then directed appealing eyes at Gruber's face.

"VON BERNE is dead, *Fuehrer*," he said in a quivering voice. "And I am at loss how to explain it. We were to fly off shore and meet the U-Sixteen for a test cruise this morning, but when I went to von Berne's place he was gone. A few hours later I learned of an airplane accident on the south coast of England. I investigated. There had been two in the plane, von Berne and somebody else. A British pilot saw them in the air, and it was his report to the Air Ministry I managed to hear. He said that von Berne and the other man were fighting in the plane... the plane von Berne and I were to fly out to the U-Sixteen. The stranger jumped, his parachute was torn, and his body exploded when he struck the ground. He...."

"What?" Gruber screamed. "Exploded? You mean...?"

The German *Fuehrer* was so excited and furious he couldn't control his voice. Spittle drooled down from one corner of his mouth. The civilian spy nodded and looked more unhappy than ever.

"I am afraid so, my *Fuehrer*," he said. "Von Berne had prepared enough of Formula Q for the test cruise with the U-Sixteen. We had selected the Plymouth naval base. I had completed an accurate chart of those waters. I...."

"This other man with von Berne?" Peiplow thundered. "Who was he? What was he doing with von Berne?"

"I do not know, *Herr* Peiplow," the other said meekly. "But, if you will let me finish? Von Berne managed to get his plane down, but crashed. He must have been badly wounded in the battle. The British pilot landed close and pulled him from the burning plane. Von Berne tried to shoot him, then died. But there is something else, something I was unable to find out."

"What?" Gruber hissed at him.

"Just a rumor," the other said. "A rumor that von Berne said things before he realized that this Captain Combat was not...."

"Combat?" Gruber shrilled, and started pounding his fists on Peiplow's desk top. "That American dog? That *Schweinehund? Mein Gott*, is there not one loyal German who can remove that swine from my life? Von Berne really spoke to *him?*"

"It is only a rumor, my *Fuehrer,*" the civilian spy said. "I was unable to find out for sure. In the light of what had happened, I thought it best to contact Number Thirty-Six at once and have him fly me here direct."

A deathly silence settled over the room, then Gruber suddenly broke it with a sound like air escaping from a tire.

"To report to me direct, eh?" he snarled at the quaking spy. "To report—what? Complete failure! Were not your orders to guard von Berne with your life? He was in charge of the Formula Q affair in England, and you were to guard him and his secret."

"Yes, yes, my *Fuehrer!*" the other wailed. "But...."

"Silence, you swine traitor!" Gruber screamed. "It is not your fault that the entire secret has not been discovered by the British. Perhaps even now they know something of it. Swine dog, you have failed in your duty to me and to the Reich! There is no excuse for failure, and there is but one penalty."

Tears gushed from the civilian spy's eyes as he dropped to his knees and begged for his life. The German *Fuehrer* spat on him, then took Peiplow's Luger from its holster and shot the man three times through the head.

"Take the dead scum away!" he shrilled and threw Peiplow's gun down on the desk.

PEIPLOW NODDED at Number Thirty-six and Khole. They picked up the dead man by the arms and dragged his body out through the steel door. They returned in a couple of minutes, and by then Gruber had his anger under partial control.

"If I may make a suggestion, my *Fuehrer?*" Number Thirty-Six said quietly.

"And that would be?" Gruber snapped.

The pilot hesitated as though choosing his words carefully. "I now outrank all agents in the British Isles," he said eventually. "And I also have a well-established place in the British Air Ministry. I would suggest that the *Fuehrer* turn over all Formula Q work to me. I have worked with von Berne right from the start, and I know all of his contacts."

"And just what would you do?"

The pilot known as Number Thirty-Six hesitated again, then took a deep breath and spoke earnestly for five full minutes. The German *Fuehrer* heard him, flint-eyed, to the very end, but when the pilot had finished he smiled slightly.

"Excellent, Number Thirty-Six," he said. "Your plan is very good, and you have my full permission to carry it through. I shall issue orders for all branches of my armed forces to cooperate with you to the fullest extent. When you have been successful you may expect the highest honor I have to bestow upon a gallant and loyal German. As usual we will contact each other at Zone K, if you need further instructions."

"Thank you, *Fuehrer!*" Number Thirty-Six beamed. "And there is one thing which I shall first prove to you can be done."

"And that?" Gruber asked with a frown.

"This Captain Combat," the man said with a deadly smile. "He has lived much too long. And there is one German who can stop him from living any longer. Myself!"

"Good, good!" Gruber shouted, and pounded the desk for emphasis. "Then all is settled. Do your work, Number Thirty-Six. I have selected April Ninth as the day."

The *Fuehrer* paused, then shot one fist above his head.

"April ninth!" he shrilled. "The first day of England's doom!"

And a hoarse cheer echoed from mouth to mouth.

CHAPTER 3
MYSTERY OF
THE MISSING MAN

SIR JOHN DRAKE, head of the British Counter-espionage Bureau, drew a hand across his worry-wrinkled brow and sighed heavily.

"You're sure he didn't say something else that you may have forgotten in the excitement?" he asked Bill Combat, who sat across the desk from him.

"If he did, then I've forgotten it for keeps, Sir John," the Yank replied promptly. "Seriously, though, I'm dead sure I've given you every word he said before he tried to snake out that Luger and nail me."

"Thankless beggar, wasn't he," the chief grunted. "You were damn lucky. And let me add, England is fortunate that he is dead. He—his name was von Berne—was one of three men who have done more damage to England's fighting forces than all the rest of the German nation put together. If we could but catch the other two, I'd sleep a whole lot better nights, I can tell you."

Combat started to speak but decided against it. This wasn't the first time that Sir John, the aged-looking but extremely clever spy catcher, had called him in for help, and he knew that if he but held his peace, he would get the whole story eventually. Sir John was like that, and absolutely nothing could be done about it. The Yank lighted a cigarette, leaned back comfortably in his chair, and waited. He didn't have to wait long; only long enough for Sir John to get an evil-smelling pipe stoked up.

"You might call it fate that made you take that flight this morning, Combat," the older man began in his own good time. "I mean, that at the very time you were in the air I was having an order sent to your Colonel for you to report to me here. Yes, oddly enough, I wanted to see you about the two occupants of that sport plane. That was, of course, before they died. Well, my story isn't very long—for the reason I know so confounded little about it. I'll give you the facts I have, though."

Sir John paused to get his dead pipe started again, then promptly forgot all about it as he leaned forward on the desk.

"What I'm telling you now, Combat," he said, "happened a good three months before the German *Fuehrer* even sent his goose-stepping killers into Austria. And, for reasons you'll understand as I go along, not one single word of it appeared in print in any paper in the world. It was this: the disappearance here in England of a man named Frankle, Varden Frankle. Have you ever heard of him?"

"No," Combat said and shook his head. "The name sounds Austrian to me."

"Correct," Sir John nodded. "He was born in Vienna some sixty-two years ago. He grew up to be a great chemist, but an extraordinarily eccentric one. In a way, you might call him the first real flesh and blood, honest to goodness pacifist. He hated all war, and it was his life's ambition to develop a powerful chemical weapon and present it—free—to every nation on the face of the earth. Yes, he truly believed that if all nations could possess this deadly weapon, they would not dare wage war against each other for fear of annihilation. In short, there would be no strong and weak nations. They would all be equally strong, defensively."

"A swell idea if it would work," Combat grinned.

"Varden Frankle had high hopes," Sir John said. "However, along came Nineteen Fourteen, and the German Kaiser started out to try and conquer the world. His staff, of course, knew of Frankle, and they tried to draft him into forced chemical warfare service. Frankle refused, fled Germany by the skin of his teeth, and took refuge here in England. He has been here ever since, and...."

Sir John paused, leaned forward even more and pressed both fists hard against the top of his desk.

"And did develop a secret explosive—credited with being

fifty times more powerful than anything else known to man!" he said in what was almost an awed whisper. "That much we know definitely. But what it is composed of, what its formula is, we do not know. This explosive—known as Formula Q—was to be his present to England and her allies. I believe that when Hitler gobbled up his Austria, and beloved Vienna, Frankle forsook his life's ambition in favor of avenging his Austria against the Nazis. Anyway, England and her allies were to be given the secret formula in case Hitler started riding roughshod across the face of the world. The War Office has that promise in writing. And some six months ago, two high War Office officials attended a secret demonstration of his discovery. That is what I mean when I say we definitely know how powerful it is." The British counter-espionage chief stopped once more, swore sharply and rapped his clenched fist on the desk.

"AND THEN suddenly he disappeared with all of his data and experimental materials!" he snapped harshly. "Every Intelligence man in England, and the police, went on the job of finding Varden Frankle. We didn't find a trace of him until about three weeks ago. And here my story becomes spotty. I can't give you the exact truth, because I don't know it. The man who knows the truth is gone. You saw him fall to his death with a ripped parachute this morning."

"You mean that he must have had…?" Combat blurted out before he could check himself.

"I mean just that!" Sir John said gravely. "From your report, and the statements of those on the ground who saw his fall, I am convinced that he had some of Varden Frankle's Formula Q explosive on his person. And here is something else, the most distressing thing of all to me. That man was the best Intelligence agent in our service. His name was Roberts, and it was he who all alone managed to get on the trail of the missing Frankle. He got wind of the story while on another job in Germany. He completed that job and returned to England and went to work on the Frankle case. The trail led to three men. One was von Berne—who tried to kill you today. The other was a George Crater—von Berne's assistant in spy work here in England. The third was one we regard as the mystery man of Germany. We don't even know his name, or what he looks like. We only know that he goes under the title of Number Thirty-Six. Von Berne, Crater, and this Number Thirty-Six, are the three I spoke of as having done England the most damage."

"But you've known who von Berne and Crater were all along?" Combat asked amazed.

"Only since Roberts returned from Germany," Sir John said. "At his request they were not picked up. He was to keep tabs on them. He also hoped to lead us to this mysterious Number Thirty-Six. It may seem strange that I gave Roberts such a free hand. I did because he alone found out that Varden Frankle had been kidnapped and was a German agent's prisoner somewhere *here* in the British Isles. And he has been making his Formula Q explosive under the direction of that German agent, who Roberts was convinced was von Berne."

"Making it?" Combat cried. "But good Lord, Sir John, a plant big enough to turn out explosives in any quantity could be tracked down, and...."

21

"And you are dead wrong, Combat," the other cut in quietly. "That was the most remarkable thing about Formula Q, according to our War Office experts' reports. A mere pound of it could blow the HMS Rodney right out of the water. No, Formula Q could be made in a space no bigger than a one car garage. It looked something like red clay, I have been told, and could be moulded by a Frankle process into any size or shape. He conducted the War Office demonstration with pellets no bigger than your little fingernail. And the strangest thing of all was the way it was exploded. Not by heat, detonation, or an electric current, but by the friction of one piece of Formula Q striking another!"

"Good God!" Combat breathed. "That poor devil Roberts must have had some in his pocket!"

"Quite likely," Sir John nodded, "but we'll probably never know. However, that brings me close to the end of this spotty story. Yesterday Roberts sent through word to me that he was reporting today with the whole story. He did not report today. Obviously he caught hold of something very important having to do with von Berne, and did not dare leave. Von Berne is dead, Roberts is dead, Crater has disappeared but will be instantly arrested if he is found, which somehow I doubt. This Number Thirty-Six is as much of a mystery as ever. And I still don't know definitely where Frankle is being kept a prisoner."

Combat stiffened slightly and gave Sir John a keen look.

"Just what do you mean by *not definitely?*" he asked.

"FOR THE past week," Sir John said, slowly, "Roberts has been sending all his code messages through from the mountain section around Forsinard in the northern tip of Scotland. He did not even trust to the code, so his reports were like this story I've been telling you, very spotty indeed, with much I'd like to know missing. But they did contain a strong hint that Frankle was up there someplace."

"And you want me to find Frankle," Combat finished.

"More than that," Sir John said grimly. "Roberts had hold of something gigantic, else he would have sent for help rather than come down here in person to report to me. In other words— and this, of course, you can call a wild guess—Roberts found out the whole truth but didn't dare take drastic steps until he had conferred with me. Things moved too fast for him, however, and he didn't have the *chance* to confer with me. He was forced to stick close to this von Berne, for some reason… and died."

Finishing the last with a heavy sigh, Sir John returned once again to his un-lighted pipe. Combat made no effort to speak. He sat perfectly still, milling over his own thoughts. They were not particular happy ones.

With Roberts dead, the mystery of Varden Frankle was just about as much of a mystery as ever.

"I know exactly what you are thinking, Combat," Sir John suddenly broke into the Yank's spell of disheartening reverie, "and I'll admit that it seems completely and utterly hopeless. Also, perhaps a little on the crazy side to you, eh? If I believe that Frankle is up there somewhere near Forsinard, why not have the entire section combed, eh?"

"I was going to bring that point up, Sir John," Combat nodded and grinned faintly. "I don't mean that I wouldn't tackle any job you gave me. When I saw the lousy Nazis murder my uncle, Lord Brainbridge—in Posen, Poland—the day before war broke out, I swore I'd carry on as well as I know how, if for no other reason than out of respect for his memory. He was your close friend, he did War Office work with you for years, so you have only to ask me anything, Sir John, and I'll try my damnedest. However, I was thinking of the quickest way to clear up this mystery."

"**THE BEST** and quickest way is for one man to tackle it alone," Sir John said evenly. "I have a couple of hundred damn fine agents I could assign to the job, but I prefer you to try it. You smashed the Nazi effort to break the British North Sea blockade, and you spoiled Germany's November Eleventh attempt to *Blitzkrieg* right through Holland to the English Channel. I believe the mystery of Formula Q and Varden Frankle is equally important to the future of England. Remember, one pound of Formula Q will blow a battleship clean out of the water. Remember, too, that Formula Q is being made right here in the British Isles. Why? *Because it is going to be used right here!* Good God, there is no limit to what Nazi agents here in England could do! We've got to find Frankle—and not even let the Nazi agents suspect that we are looking for him. A hundred men combing that area would be noticed, but you...."

Sir John stopped short as a wall buzzer sounded. He pushed a desk button and looked at the side door. A Bureau officer entered and silently handed Sir John a slip of yellow paper. The chief of counterespionage frowned and pulled open a desk drawer and took out a small black book.

"Have a cigarette," he grunted at Combat. "This type of message I decode myself."

Combat had smoked two cigarettes before Sir John looked up from the message. The man's face had suddenly become drawn and haggard, but there was a glint of savage determination in his eyes.

"Perhaps we are too late," he said in a husky voice, and tapped the slip of yellow paper with a pencil point. "An hour ago the British submarine *Swordfish* was blown up and sunk at her dock in the Plymouth naval base. A candy peddler tossed a bag of candy to one of the sailors. It hit the desk and blew open the bow. The peddler tried to run away and was shot dead by the base sentries. That peddler has sold candy there at Plymouth for years. Today he sold death under his true colors—not candy, but Formula Q!"

"It's like a mad, crazy nightmare," Combat said in a hard voice.

"That is exactly what that dog Gruber wants to make this war like—to the whole civilized world," Sir John said.

Combat nodded slowly, then crushed out his cigarette and rose to his feet.

"Any suggestions or instructions, Sir John?" he asked quietly.

"None, save arrangements I have made, which you can reject if you think of a better plan of attack," the Bureau chief said. "Naturally, you can cover more territory by plane than on foot. To make your going to the north of Scotland perfectly regular, I have arranged for your assignment as a fledgling pilot to the Fifty-Ninth Coastal Patrol Squadron at Wick on the Scottish coast, less than thirty-five miles from Forsinard. Wick will at least serve as a base from which you can work. Incidentally, you are going north as Lieutenant Cramer. The name Combat is too well known throughout the Air Force."

"That's as good a way as any to start," Combat shrugged. "I only hope I'll be able to do some good."

"That will be my nightly prayer from this moment on," Sir John said grimly. "Overlook nothing, and be on your guard constantly. Nazi agents are everywhere, and they'll go to any limits to guard the secret of Formula Q. In this war you can be sure of nothing. I pray to Heaven it isn't so, Combat, but there is the possibility that you may go out that door straight to your death."

And though neither Sir John Drake nor Captain Bill Combat heard them, the war gods up yonder loudly agreed that such was a damn *good* possibility.

CHAPTER 4
DEATH IN THE DARK

SOME FIFTEEN minutes after leaving Sir John's office, Combat paid off the cab driver in front of the "diggings" he maintained in London. They were located on the top floor of a four story rooming house in the West End, just off Piccadilly. For a couple of moments he stood on the sidewalk, watching the cab pick its way along the more or less blacked-out street. During the ride up from the War Office he had mulled over everything that had been told him. He felt very pessimistic about the whole thing and actually regretted that Sir John had handed him the job. When boiled right down to bare facts, he didn't have a single thing to go on save Sir John's firm belief that Frankle was being held prisoner somewhere in the Forsinard section of Scotland. That could mean something, but more likely it could mean absolutely nothing.

Yet, as he stood watching the cab disappear from view, a sudden change stole over him. It was a feeling he could not define, a hunch similar to that which had caused him to take the Hurricane aloft for a test flight some nine hours ago. He started to laugh it off, but he checked the laugh as beads of cold sweat suddenly oozed out on his forehead.

"I must be getting a bad case of nerves," he growled, and swung up the steps of his rooming house. "Or maybe I just need a couple of stiff drinks. Yeah, that should fill the bill."

They didn't, however. They increased the eerie sensation in him, if anything. He decided against a third drink and grimly went about changing the rank insignia on his uniform from that of a captain to a fledgling lieutenant. He was to pick up his replacement ship at Hendon first thing in the morning, or sooner if he wished. He wished it to be sooner. A night in London with these damn jitters wouldn't help at all.

"I'm a first class sap, acting this way!" he snarled at himself. "My God, I..." He stopped short, his mouth still open. At that moment his eyes happened to focus on the door of the closet where he kept his civilian clothes to wear when on leave, and a couple of spare uniforms. It was locked, but there were marks in the wood close to the lock indicating that it had been jimmied open. He moved over to them, studied them intently. He took out a key to unlock the door, but an alarm suddenly sounded in his brain. There was no sane reason why he shouldn't, but something told him not to open that door.

He stood looking at the jimmy marks, and suddenly the eerie sensation surged through him stronger than ever. In that second he would have sworn that eyes were watching him. He even imagined his back burned where those unseen eyes bored into it. He had the crazy urge to laugh harshly and show up his own damn foolish feeling by opening the door. But there was that cautioning note in him that was stronger, and he forced himself to turn away from the door.

As he did he shot a quick but careless-appearing glance at the row of three windows at the back of his room. They looked out onto a fire-escape. Did his eyes play him tricks, or was that the darker shadow of a man slipping back from one corner of the left window? His skin began to prickle all over, and the roof of his mouth went dry. Eyes *had* been watching him. Of that he was positive, now. The damn war was even smoking him out in the little flat he kept in London.

Who, why, and for what reason, he had no idea, but he knew that death lurked in that locked closet, and that death also lurked out there beyond the window on the fire-escape. And if he was going to go on living he had to act—and act damn fast. Thought and action became one for Combat. He stooped over as though to brush something off the toe of his shoe. Instead, though, he dropped the tunic he was still holding and caught up a small footstool. In what was practically a continuation of the same

SCENE OF THIS STORY

movement, he flung the footstool straight at the one floor lamp that was lighted. He scored a bullseye. The light bulb went *pop,* and the room was instantly plunged into, darkness.

But not before his steel grey eyes had caught the movement of the window to the left being raised an inch.

IN PRACTICALLY the same instant, he was again in furious motion. One swift leap brought him to the reading table on the far side of the room. He'd placed his holstered service gun there after taking it off. He grabbed it up, holster and all, and drilled two quick shots at the bottom half of the left window. Glass tinkled and there was a muffled curse, then two stabs of orange red flame spurted back at him. Rather, they spurted back at where he had been a couple of split seconds before. By then he had raced toward the foyer door that led outside into the hall.

By some damn fast moving he hoped to get up onto the roof from where he would have the fire-escape prowler caught cold. But he never reached the roof. As he jerked open the foyer door, he suddenly crashed headlong into a lurking figure outside. A harsh voice said something he didn't get, and a knee dug deep into his belly. White pain engulfed him and for a second he couldn't move a muscle.

Shoulders were lowered and they came butting into his chest, to send him hurling back into the room. Somehow, though, he had managed to turn his body slightly. The charging figure slid off him, lost balance, and went stumbling blindly into the dark room. A scream of terror and the crack of a gun shattered the darkness inside.

"No, no, Karl, hold your fire!"

By then Combat had spun all the way around. The hall light shed a dim glow through the opened foyer door and back into his room. He saw that his window was raised all the way up and that the head and shoulders of a man were protruding through into the room. The figure's face was turned so that Combat couldn't see it. He could see the Luger, however, and he blinked in confusion as he saw that the gun was pointed toward the door of his clothes closet.

It all seemed to happen in the flicker of a single second. The man leaning in the window pumped three shots at the closet door. The person who had stumbled into the room and fallen flat was screaming in terror and struggling desperately to twist around and crawl back into the hall. And at the same time, Combat ripped up his own gun and drilled two slugs into the skull of the man leaning in through the window.

Then the whole house seemed to topple in a terrific roar of sound. The concussion from the exploding red hell inside Combat's room seemed virtually to pick up the crawling man on the floor and hurl him out into the hall. His head hit hard against the door jamb and cracked like an eggshell.

Combat had only time to see the man's body sailing through the air toward him before a terrific blast of hot air slapped into him and knocked his legs out from under him. Instinctively he flung out his two hands to grab anything for support, but they clutched only thin air and he stumbled backwards off the top step of the flight of stairs. In a sea of hot air and acrid smelling smoke, he went tumbling head over heels down those stairs. There was just enough sense left in his blast-stunned brain to cause him to jackknife his body and bury his head and face in his arms, but even then it seemed as though giant hammers pounded every square inch of his body.

When he finally bounced to a stop on the third floor landing, he was too winded and smashed around to do anything but lay there, huddled and struggling grimly to fight off the wave of blissful unconsciousness that tried to engulf him. Shouts and cries rang in his ears. Footsteps pounded unheeded past him, and from a long way off he heard the sharp crackle of flames. It was the sound of those flames and their red glare penetrating his blurred eyes that eventually snapped him into action and got him up on his feet.

IT WAS like finding himself in a roaring red hell. The whole top floor of the rooming house was on fire. People who had gone rushing up to see what had happened were now piling down past him, screaming. In their frenzied excitement not a single person seemed to notice him, let alone speak to him, and as his brain cleared a bit he was truly thankful. The one important thing now was to get out of that house unnoticed. Things had begun to click in his brain, and he wanted to get in touch with Sir John Drake at once.

He charged through the hall full of milling people and went down the three flights of stairs to the street. More people were outside, and in the distance he could hear the sound of London's fire engines. Slowing up his pace slightly, he shouldered his way through the group of pop-eyed onlookers and made tracks toward a taxi rank, three blocks down. As luck would have it, there was a lone cab at the stand. He started to climb inside but the driver, after a quick look at his disheveled appearance, thrust out a barring arm.

"Hold on there, mate!" the driver cried. "What's all this about? Who you running away from, eh?"

Combat slapped the barring arm aside and leaped into the car.

"Air Force business!" he barked into the driver's face. "Emergency! Get me to the War Office, and step on it!"

"Oh!" the driver gulped, and geared the car into motion so fast that Combat was flung back on the seat.

It seemed as though the cab driver had no sooner shifted into high than he jammed on the brakes and skidded to a halt in front of London's very unimpressive looking War Office. Yelling at the driver to wait, Combat leaped out and bounced up the stone steps. Inside the double doors two guards, and a civilian obviously from Scotland Yard, jumped on him and pinned him fast.

But before he could even get his mouth open to protest one of the guards recognized him.

"Blimey!" the man gasped. "It's Captain Combat! Lord, sir, what's happened to you?"

"Tell you later, Sergeant," Combat said hurriedly. "Right now I've got to see Sir John. He's in his office?"

"He is that, sir," said the guard sergeant in a sober voice. "But he's dead."

Combat jerked to a quick halt and wheeled back.

"He's what?" he practically shouted.

"He's dead, sir," the sergeant repeated. "He was shot to death about fifteen minutes after you left, sir. They got the dirty beggar what done it; one of Sir John's clerks in the outer office. The stinker killed himself, though, before they could get his gun away. But what happened to you, sir?"

Combat didn't answer. In that moment the building lobby started to whirl around and around. He staggered a few steps and leaned weakly against a stone pillar for support. He had the sudden mad impression that the entire world had dropped away from under his feet. A ten year old school kid could figure the truth, now. He turned his head and looked at the guard sergeant.

"Do you know, Sergeant?" he said with an effort. "Do you know if they found a dictograph concealed in his office?"

The non-com's eyes flew open wide with surprise.

"That they did, sir!" the man exclaimed. "Right underneath his desk it was. How did you guess, Captain?"

One again Combat ignored the man's questions. His head was too full of other thoughts. Someone had listened in while Sir John had told him of Robert's secret reports, and Sir John's deductions from these reports. Some one knew that he, Combat, was heading for the northern tip of Scotland to try to pick up the threads that death had wrenched from Roberts' hands. And so Sir John had been murdered, and an attempt had been made to snuff out his own life. He would probably never know for sure, but he would always believe that a Formula Q death trap had been waiting for him behind that closet door in his room.

Some evil master mind had laid his plans well, and only by a miracle of miracles had not the only two men who knew the details of the Formula Q mystery *both* been removed from the world. One had, but he, Combat, still lived. Yet Sir John had not died in vain. His death was now concrete proof that what he had firmly believed *was* true. Varden Frankle *was* somewhere up there at the tip of Scotland.

"And when they killed Sir John, they proved it to me, the stinking rats!" Combat grated aloud.

"What's that, sir?" the guard sergeant asked.

"Just thinking out loud," Combat said. Then, leveling a keen glance at the three of them, he said, "If you want to honor the memory of Sir John, and do England a great service, make no mention to *anyone* that I came back here. Understand?"

"Perfectly, sir," the three of them answered together.

"Thanks," Combat nodded, and swung around and went out the door.

CHAPTER 5
MIDNIGHT MURDER

COLONEL STAFFORD, of the British Home Air Base at Hendon, glanced up from the paper he held in his hand and nodded at the tall fledgling lieutenant who stood at attention before him. A dry smile split his lips.

"Anxious to get on active duty, eh, Lieutenant Cramer?" he grunted. "Well, can't blame you. Was like that myself in the last mess. See Sergeant Baker in Hangar Four. Your replacement plane is there. Good luck."

"Thank you, sir," Lieutenant (Combat) Cramer replied, and saluted smartly.

Ten minutes later the Yank-born R.A.F. ace sat in the cockpit of a Supermarine Spitfire waiting for it to warm up. There was a look of grim, savage determination in his steel blue eyes, but it did not exactly check with the thoughts passing through his head. Damn the guy who invented the dictograph, anyway! That lousy little gadget had told his unknown and unseen enemy....

"Wonder if it was this mysterious Number Thirty-Six?" he broke into his own thoughts. "I hope some day I meet the louse face to face."

He clenched one fist and rapped it on the joystick for emphasis and returned to his thoughts. The dictograph had told his unknown enemy that he was going to join the Fifty-Ninth at Wick, then search for the secret hideout where Varden Frankle was being kept a prisoner. Of course, if they believed him to have died in his room explosion he would at least have a few hours jump on them before they started checking his presence at Fifty-Nine. However, he wished he didn't have to go to Fifty-Nine as Fledgling Cramer. But there wasn't anything else to do about it.

For with Sir John dead, he alone knew of the Formula Q secret—at least, as much of the secret as the dead Roberts had given to Sir John before he jumped to his death. And the north of Scotland was his hunting ground. He had to take a chance and go to Fifty-Nine as Cramer, because he was expected. He couldn't very well report and say, *"I'm not Cramer, I'm Joe Glutz. Cramer said he didn't care about flying, and that I could come here in his place."*

To ease off the jumble of conflicting thoughts that plagued his brain, he took from his pocket a small but very clear picture of Varden Frankle that Sir John had given him. It had been taken at the time of the visit of the War Office experts and

showed a thin, wrin-
kle-faced little man
with hardly any hair,
yet with great bushy
white eyebrows that
almost hid his eyes.
Combat studied
every detail of the
face until they were
indelibly stamped
on his brain, then
he tore the picture
into countless small
pieces and let the

propwash carry them whipping and whirling across the Hendon
field.

By then the Spitfire was ready to go. He signaled the officer in
the control tower that he was ready and waiting for an all-clear
runway. Easing off the wheel brakes, he taxied out to the head
of the runway, got a final "go-ahead" from the control tower
officer, and opened up his engine. Like a race horse breaking
from the barrier, the Spitfire shot forward, picked up take-off
speed in practically nothing flat, and went roaring up toward
the star-dotted heavens under Combat's skilled, steady touch.

CIRCLING THE field until he was fifteen thousand feet
above it, Combat then checked his radio with the ground
station. They gave him the weather clear, north to the Orkney
Islands. That is, the ground station gave him the weather in code

and wished him good luck in plain, every day English. Thanking them, Combat banked north, set his ship on a bee-line course, then relaxed in the seat.

For the ten thousandth time he mulled over the events of the past day. When he had finished, two unanswerable questions stood out above all else.

"First," he started to ponder them aloud, "if Frankle hates *Der Fuehrer's* guts so, how come he's turning out Formula Q for his agents? Is it because they've got him fooled, or do they know the secret of Formula Q, and is Frankle already dead? Second, why just sink *one* sub at Plymouth? Why not hold back for something big? Sinking that sub was just the same as telling the British they are making supplies of Formula Q. Nuts, it just doesn't add up to make sense. Here's hoping it will when, and *if,* I find Varden Frankle."

He guided the Spitfire northward and slightly west, toward Fifty-Nine's field at Wick. But when he was just about to cut across the imaginary line between England and Scotland, another plane suddenly came slashing down out of the heavens at him. Aerial machine guns yammered out their savage song and countless messengers of death went ripping past his wings.

The attack came from behind him and above, but he didn't twist around in the seat to take a look. Experience had taught him that such inquisitiveness could cost a man his life. He did the only safe and sane thing a man could do under the circumstances. He hammered the Spitfire up, over and down in a flash half roll, let it engine-howl earthward for a thousand feet or so, and then hauled it upward in a wide, prop-clawing, climbing turn.

Then and only then did he turn in the seat and cast his gaze about the dark heavens for a look at his attacker. A silhouette sliding across a strip of stars rewarded his search. He couldn't make out the type or nationality, because the distance was too great. However, he dismissed the sudden thought that it might be a Nazi plane. He was pretty sure it was a pursuit ship, and for a Nazi pursuit job to fly all the way across the North Sea and give him battle, it would have to be fitted with extra gas tanks from wing-tip to wingtip. And it wouldn't have been able to get off the ground with such a load, in the first place.

"Nope, some dizzy R.A.F. lad on night patrol," he grunted aloud, and watched the silhouetted ship start to curve over and down. "Wish to hell I knew his wave length. I'd radio him a few choice words that would blow up his damn tubes in his face. Here comes the fool again!"

The other ship was now coming down again like a bat out of hell. Face set, Combat held his course until the last second. Then with a yell he whipped his ship through a pretzel maneuver that left the other pilot shooting at nothing but thin air. And as Combat raced up past the ship he saw that it was a British Hawker Hurricane. Kicking rudder, he swung around over the plane, then shot his nose down and drilled a long burst across the other's wing. Then he cut his fire, swung in close, and shook a fist at the dim huddle of black shadow that was the pilot hunched in the other pit.

"You damn truck driver, are you blind?" he bellowed into his own roaring engine. "Take a look, blast your hide!"

AS COMBAT spoke the last, he whipped out his free hand and snapped on his wing lights. In their sudden brilliance his ship's markings stood out in clear relief. Then he snapped them off again. As he veered off, he saw the other pilot waggle his wings in a gesture of acknowledgment, and go veering off in the opposite direction. Combat cursed him through clenched teeth and put his Spitfire back on its course northward. That is, he started to put it on its course.

The Hawker Hurricane had streaked around in a dime turn, and was tearing in at him again, all guns blazing!

For a split second Combat was too amazed to move. And in that same second he could have reached out and shaken hands with the Grim Reaper himself. As a matter of fact, death came within an ace of slapping him right in the face. Hot bullets smashed through his cockpit's glass cowling as though it was so much paper. An invisible finger plucked at the collar of his flying suit, and there was a tinkle of glass as the face of the altimeter on the instrument panel was shattered and mashed into a glob of useless junk.

By then, however, Combat had snapped out of his trance and was kicking his Spitfire out into the clear with absolutely no regard for structural strength of the wings. He made it, though, and the wings didn't come off. Eyes bright and brittle, he hauled the ship up in a half loop, slammed it off the top, and streaked straight downward like the hammers of hell.

The Hurricane pilot saw him coming and tried to dive down

and completely lose himself in the darkness. However, he had a veteran of war-torn skies on his tail, and that veteran was sore as hell for being picked on twice in the same night. As a result the Hurricane pilot might just as well have tried to jump out and slide down a pole as try to fly away from that wild, American-born eagle above him.

"You saw my markings!" Combat shouted as he closed in on the other ship. "You know damn well I'm British. So my guess is, *you're not!* And that makes me curious. Go on. Get down there and land, or so help me I'll shoot you right out of that crate!"

As he spoke the last, he slapped a couple of warning bursts down close by the other ship. When he had started his dive, red rage had filled him with but one purpose—to shoot the man down. That rage was mostly gone now, and cold logic was in charge of his actions. If the Hurricane pilot really was some fat-headed R.A.F. pilot who couldn't tell a British ship from a Nazi job, Combat didn't want to have mistaken murder on his soul. Also, if the pilot belonged to the rat group who had slain Sir John and had tried to do the same to him, he wanted to capture the man alive. There might be a chance of making him talk.

Combat stuck to the other plane like a leech. A dozen times the other pilot tried to slice off and speed away, but each time the Yank was right on top of him like a stalking tiger and hammering short bursts through the other's wings—much too damn close for that gentleman's comfort. All the time a tiny fear quivered in Combat's brain. It was the fear that the other pilot would suddenly decide to fight it out rather than submit.

But as the two planes roared nearer and nearer to the night-shadowed earth below, and the other pilot made no attempt to give serious battle, Combat became more and more convinced that his hunch was correct. The other pilot was a Nazi agent, because that was the only breed of snake in the world who would give up rather than chance losing its life in an even fight.

However, as the Hurricane came down to within five hundred feet of the ground, its pilot made one last effort to slice away to safety. The man's fears were greater than his flying ability, however. Combat cursed savagely and held his fire, because there was no need of slapping a warning burst down at the other ship. The force of gravity, and a plane with wings weakened by crazy flying, were taking care of that little thing for him.

IN OTHER words, the other pilot didn't figure on his terrific diving speed and tried to pull out too fast. He did get the nose up a hair, but in that exact second one half of the right wing buckled back and let go. As though some invisible giant had reached a hand down out of the night sky and twisted the ship like a kid's top, the Hurricane suddenly whirled around and around, and all the time sank belly first toward the ground.

Peering down through the bad lights, Combat eased back his own throttle and came out of his dive a bit and watched the other fight fruitlessly against the terrific centrifugal force set up by the plane. Four times the man managed to force himself up on the seat of his ship. But each time he was unable to bail out over the side and go down the rest of the way by parachute. Centrifugal force held him in the cockpit as though he were nailed there.

The spinning ship smacked down into a cluster of trees and crashed and bounced down through them to the ground. Combat groaned and waited to see the sheet of flame belch upward, but no fire came. The pilot had either cut his ignition in plenty of time, or else the gods of war had decided that Combat at least deserved *this* much of a break. The Yank, however, didn't give a thought to that angle of the affair. The instant he was convinced that flames were not going to spoil the party for him, he snapped on his lights and spotted a good field right next to the clump of trees.

In practically nothing flat he had landed and was racing through the beams of his landing lights to the heap of crumpled wreckage under the trees. As he neared it, a bit of common sense suddenly popped into his head and he veered sharply out of the beams of his lights and drew his service automatic from its holster. There was no sense sticking his face right into a second close call, such as he had had with von Berne on England's south coast early that morning.

And so he approached the wreck from the side. However, when he was close enough, he saw there was no reason for worry. The pilot was jammed tight in the smashed cockpit and it was easy to see that both arms were broken in a dozen places and were utterly useless. The man was not dead yet, though the bleak light in his eyes told Combat that the cold breath of death was close. The rear of the engine had slammed back and virtually crushed the man's chest to a pulp.

He could still hear, however, for the sound of Combat's approaching footsteps caused him to turn his head. For a moment the bleak stare of death's nearness left the man's eyes, and they became as von Berne's eyes had been that morning— livid with stark, bestial hatred. His bleeding lips moved, sprayed froth, and a hoarse whisper came from between them.

"Thirty-Six will get you yet, swine!" he hissed. "He has so promised *Der Fuehrer.* And Thirty-Six never fails!"

Combat stepped closer and eyed the man coldly.

"You're through, Nazi," he said. "You don't want to burn in hell, do you? Maybe you can atone for what you've been—what your *Fuehrer* has made of you—by doing one good turn for the decent men in this world. Where is Varden Frankle? Just exactly where can I find him? And what is the big thing you plan to do with Formula Q?"

But Combat's plea failed utterly. The man spat bloody froth at him and sneered.

"You will never know!" he choked, "for soon Thirty-Six will send you to me. And Formula Q? The rest of your swine comrades will soon find out! They…" The Nazi stopped suddenly and his whole face lighted up in wild alarm. *"Mein Gott!"* he gasped. As the words spilled from his lips he struggled desperately to lift his right arm toward the R.A.F. emblem he wore. He moved it but an inch and screamed with pain through clenched teeth. The scream acted as a dump valve that spilled out the very last drop of strength from his body. In that second death swooped down and claimed another of its own.

CHAPTER 6
MESSAGE FROM HELL

FOR SEVERAL moments Combat stood staring down into the death-chilled face, then suddenly the meaning of the German's exclamation and dying movement registered on his brain. The Nazi had obviously remembered something he'd forgotten. Something he wanted to destroy before he took his last breath.

"Is that it?" Combat spoke to the dead man. "Something you didn't want me to see?"

The Yank hesitated to go through the pockets of the blood-soaked tunic. Nazi though the man was, it seemed slightly on the ghoulish side to paw over the corpse. However, Combat steeled himself against the thought and grimly dug out the contents of the dead German's pockets. He found what he was looking for in the upper left tunic pocket. It was a telegram addressed to Lieutenant Jackson of the Fifty-Ninth Coastal Squadron. It had come from London. It read:

> Thinking of you tonight. Finished combat training. Hope to see you soon. Congratulations. Contact and good luck to your gallant pals in Fifty-Nine and three cheers for true blue you.
> Barry Lake.

For reasons he could not exactly explain to himself at the time, Combat was not very much surprised to learn that Lieutenant Jackson was a Nazi agent serving with the Fifty-Ninth at Wick. Somehow that seemed to be expected, now that he

45

CAPTAIN COMBAT

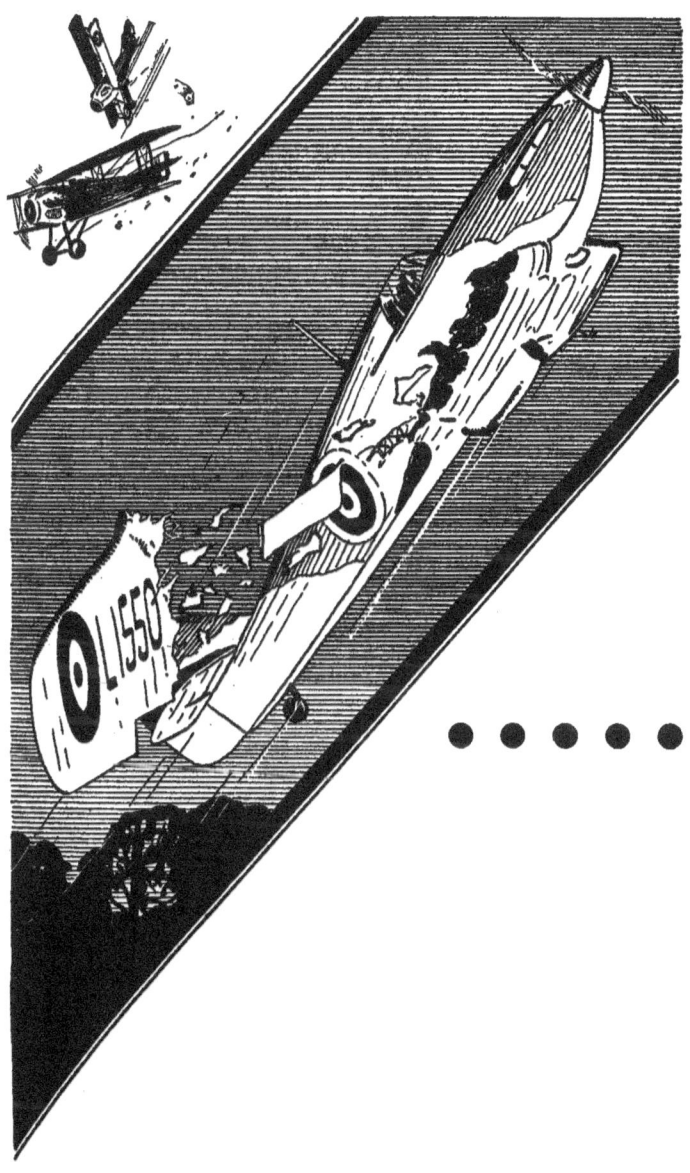

was sure some hidden spot around Forsinard was his goal. With Fifty-Nine so close to the area, it was good business for the Nazis to get one of their agents in that squadron where he could keep watch.

"And somehow my money says there's no such guy as Barry Lake," Combat grunted aloud. "A check-back to the office where this wire was handed in would probably find Lake's address a fake, too. Yeah, and… My god!"

The Yank-born eagle yelped the last because at that moment he had turned the telegram so that the brilliant glow of the plane's landing lights fell directly on it. And it was then he saw that something else had been printed in lightly with pencil between the lines of the typed wire. As he read it the back of his neck crawled and sweat broke out on his forehead. The real wire was simply code, and between the lines the dead agent had written in the real meaning of the message. And that message read:

> Go on patrol tonight. Will radio if Combat escapes us. Destroy him. Tomorrow midnight use third rowboat from left at Wick and head for trawler 'Gallant' for instructions. New countersign three cheers.
>
> Thirty-Six.

Studying the penciled words intently in hope of gaining additional meaning, Combat finally stuck the letter in his pocket and proceeded to haul the broken dead body out onto the ground. And there he searched the corpse from head to toe. But it was all to no avail. He finally stood up and wiped beads of sweat from his brow.

"Can't expect all the breaks," he grunted. "Fat chance he'd keep his code book on his person. Probably knows it by heart. But hell, it would have been nice!"

AS COMBAT walked over to his Spitfire, he saw car lights approaching and suddenly realized it wouldn't help his plans any to be found there with a dead man... a dead man wearing the uniform of the King. He vaulted into the pit, gunned the engine a bit to clear the cylinders of loggy gas, and made a quick take-off from the short, narrow field. As he roared upward for altitude he thought he heard the bark of a rifle, but he wasn't sure. He didn't wait for a second shot, if there was to be one. He went hell bent right up to ten thousand feet, leveled off and set his course once more for Fifty-Nine's field at Wick.

A little over an hour later he contacted the field's radio station, identified himself by his code number, and then circled until landing flares had been put out and he'd received the signal to come on in. Mechanics helped him taxi into the line, and he couldn't help but see their eyes pop when they suddenly spotted the bullet holes in his wings and engine cowling. Those bullet holes were going to take some explaining. And damn it all, just what would he have to say for himself when the crashed Hurricane was found and its dead pilot identified as Lieutenant Jackson from Fifty-Nine?

In spite of the value to him, he hoped, of the decoded telegram in his pocket, Combat suddenly wished very much that he had not run into one Lieutenant Jackson. He had originally planned to come north in secret; as a fledgling pilot reporting for duty. Hells bells, he couldn't have obtained more publicity if he'd had the whole Hendon-to-Wick route lined with brass bands and torchlight parades.

"But that's this lousy war," he tried to console himself as he legged down out of his ship. "A swell break one minute and a nice swift kick in the face the next. Nuts!"

"Lieutenant Cramer?" a voice suddenly asked at his side.

He looked blank and came close to shaking his head, but he had a brain wave in time and remembered.

"Yes, sir," he said to the man in Squadron Leader's uniform at his side. "Reporting from Hendon. You are Major Stark?"

"That's right, and welcome to Fifty-Nine," the C.O. said. "We see a bit of action against Nazis bombers now and again. Ah! You ran into something on the way up, Lieutenant?"

The Major had glanced at Combat's plane, and now turned his eyes to the Yank's face. Combat nodded.

"Came up the east coast, sir," he lied. "Ran into two enemy Heinkles just this side of Hull. I think I got one, but…" Combat paused and acted embarrassed. "But I've no way of confirming it, sir," he finished weakly. "It went limping out to sea. I didn't think I'd better follow it."

"Probably just as well you didn't," Major Stark grunted. "Well, the mechanics will patch up those holes. Come along to the mess and get acquainted."

The next hour or so was one of the strangest—and most uncomfortable Bill Combat had ever spent in his life. To begin with, it was the first time he had ever posed as somebody else among men of his own kind. Added to that was the damn wait for Jackson's death to be discovered and word sent up to the squadron. It didn't come.

And to top it off, there was something about Major Stark that just didn't click with Combat. The C.O. seemed to think nothing of the fact he'd had a scrap on the way up, although several of the pilots were all eager for details. Also, he had the feeling Stark was watching him all the while. In short, Combat sensed that Stark knew he had lied and was playing him as a cat plays a trapped mouse. But for what?

COMBAT ALMOST dropped his drink as a sudden thought came to him. Could it be that Jackson and Stark were both…? No, that was crazy, impossible. Maybe you can slip one of your agents into an enemy squadron, but to have him actually made the commanding officer was downright impossible. Or was it? History proved that more than one high ranking officer had been really an enemy. And he considered this mysterious Number Thirty-Six.

From what little Sir John had said, and from all that had happened to him personally, Combat could not readily brush aside the very probable fact that Number Thirty-six was a man who stood high in the British service. Dammit, he just couldn't have found out so much, and brought about such quick action if he wasn't.

And, by God, there had been one man who knew he was coming to Fifty-Nine before he even knew it himself!

That man was none other than Major Stark! Sir John had made arrangements for Fifty-Nine to receive a replacement. So if Stark *was* Number Thirty-Six, he simply had to add two and two and come up with four.

Yet that was nuts, too. Hell yes! How about the telegram to Jackson? It had been signed by Thirty-Six. Yet, hold it! Thirty-Six was a man of mystery—perhaps even to Nazi agents. Naturally he'd have it fixed for that wire to be sent from London so that Jackson would never guess that his spy boss was really his commander.

AGENT 36

"Something bothering you, Cramer? Are you sick? You look all twisted up in knots."

Combat turned his head to see Major Stark at his side, and realized that his torment of thought had slipped through to show on his face. He laughed shortly, and took a long pull on his drink before he spoke.

"Both, sir, and maybe I should be ashamed a bit," he said. "That Heinkle fight tonight. I... well, it was my first. I mean, I've never killed a man before in my life."

The C.O.'s. eyes seemed to bore straight into Combat's brain for a brief second before he smiled.

"Don't let it get you down, Lieutenant," he said quietly. Then as an after thought, "That's everybody's job in war. Have a drink?"

Combat didn't have the chance to accept. At that moment the mess door opened and a radio officer hurried inside and up to Stark. He handed the C.O. a slip of paper. The squadron major glanced at it, seemed to shoot a quick side glance at Combat, and then rapped his glass on a table close by for silence. He got it before he had to break the glass.

"One more round for a silent toast, then to bed, gentlemen," he said quietly. "Lieutenant Jackson crashed and was killed tonight, quite close to the Scottish-English line."

A low murmur of sympathy rippled from mouth to mouth, then it faded off into silence as the mess bar corporal passed from pilot to pilot to fill his glass for a silent toast to the dead. Combat felt sure the C.O.'s eyes were on him but he didn't dare look up from his glass to check. Jackson had just crashed and died? Just another plane accident? Like hell! Major Stark hadn't read out the whole radiogram, because no mention had been made of the bullet holes in Jackson's wings. The holes he, Combat, had made as he forced the Nazi agent to go down. A blind man stumbling over that wrecked plane would have seen them, and their presence would most certainly have been reported along with the report of the crash itself.

An eerie premonition of more things to come, all bad, stole through Bill Combat, And the silent toast he drank to the memory of a dead Nazi settled like so much liquid lead in his stomach.

CHAPTER 7
THE DEAD HAVE FRIENDS

DAWN WAS only a couple of hours away, and although the entire squadron had turned in before twelve, Combat had not slept a wink. In fact, he had not so much as closed his eyes. Stretched out on the cot in his dark hutment, he had made every event of the last twenty-four hours pass by in review in his mind, everlastingly seeking for some seemingly insignificant but probably highly important item that had escaped his notice up until now. He came across not one, however, and when he fitted what little he did know of the mystery into a puzzle pattern, it was only to realize more strongly than ever that he hadn't even begun to get an idea of the picture.

Of only two things was he sure, and even one of these was a trifle uncertain. He was positive that the entire Nazi secret agent service in the British Isles was out to kill him at all costs. Three murder attempts in one day is quite sufficient proof to a man that somebody doesn't love him. But if he could be that sure he was on the right track—that there were results to be obtained up here at the northern tip of Scotland, he'd feel a whole lot better.

Then, too, there was Major Stark. Damn the man for giving him ideas. He....

That unnamed quality in man which science calls the sixth sense for want of a better word, suddenly sounded its alarm in Bill Combat. He didn't see anything, nor did he hear anything. He simply knew that there was somebody standing just outside his hutment door. For a long minute he held his breath and strained his ears, but if there were any sounds, they were drowned out by the breakers of the North Sea slapping against the shore on the far side of the field.

However, his nerves would not let him laugh it off. Sliding off the cot, he picked up his service gun and flashlight and eased cat-like over to the door. For a moment he stood there, and during that moment wild imagination simmered down into truth. There *was* somebody just outside. He could hear a man breathing.

For a second he hesitated, then holding the flashlight by two fingers of his left hand, he curled the other three over the doorknob and yanked the door open. Both the flashlight and his gun were ready as he barked the order.

"Hold it steady!"

Major Stark almost fell over backward, his jaw sagged open, and one hand raised in the act of knocking on the door froze in midair. Combat lowered his gun but held his light on the C.O.'s face.

"Come in, Major," he said stepping back. "Looking for something? Sorry, but being on active service makes me jumpy."

The C.O. lowered his hand to shield his eyes.

"Awake, eh?" he grunted. "God, but you gave me a start. No wonder you're the man you are. Even sleep with your ears and eyes open, eh?"

"Meaning?" Combat said in a cold voice, but took the light off the other's eyes.

"Meaning I decided it best not to wait any longer," Major Stark said. "Switch on your table light, or come over to my hutment. Either place is good for a talk without being over-heard. *Excelsior!*"

FIFTY-NINE'S COMMANDER spoke the last in a soft whisper, and it was Combat's turn to be startled. The word, *Excelsior,* was perhaps the most guarded secret of the British Intelligence Service. It was concrete proof from one of Sir John Drake's agents to another that they both worked for the same cause. Not actually being a member of Sir John's Bureau, Combat had always considered it the highest of honors to have been informed of the Bureau's secret of secrets by Sir John. He was the only one of all the other branches of England's fighting forces who knew that word. And to hear it tossed at him from Stark's lips was akin to a six inch shell exploding in his brain.

Like a man in a trance, he stared at the C.O. a moment, then slowly backed up and switched on the small table lamp. Stark grinned at him.

"I guess Sir John suddenly decided he wanted a guardian angel to watch over you," he said. "He only told me by telephone code this evening who Cramer really was."

"This evening?" Combat echoed. "What time? After eight?"

The C.O. gave him a puzzled stare. "No," he said. "I talked with him at exactly seven-three. The time is stamped on the automatic recorder in my office, if you want to look at it. Why?"

Combat didn't answer for a moment, but a sudden tightness that had come into his chest went away at Stark's words. He had left Sir John's office at exactly seven o'clock. The guard sergeant had said the Bureau chief had been killed at seven-fif-

COMBAT

STARK

teen, fifteen minutes after he'd left. So Stark was obviously telling the truth. But....

"Didn't he call again, later?" he asked with a frown.

"No," Stark said. "Fact is I called him back at nine-one, but
I couldn't get through to him. Some blockhead said he wasn't

there and said he'd take my message. It wasn't that important, so I said I'd call again in the morning. Say, what the devil is this? Do you think I picked up a certain word just by chance?"

"Not now," Combat smiled and shook his head. "Guess I'm just a cautious guy. Besides, lots of things have happened today. One of them happened just after Sir John called you. He was shot and killed."

The best actor in the world could not have faked Major Stark's reaction to Combat's words. He was as a man slammed across the face with a baseball bat. He rocked back on his heels and clutched at the side wall for support. And the most convincing item of all was that real tears leaped into his eyes. He tried three times before he could form words.

"God, no, Combat!" he finally blurted out. "Sir John? It can't be! It just can't be. He… he was the finest man in England."

"He was, Stark," Combat nodded. "His death is a loss to all mankind. But what did he tell you when he code-phoned you?"

"He told me who you were," Stark said, a dazed, pained look still in his eyes. "He said that I was to assign you to solo patrol duty so that you could do your job as you thought best. And that I was to keep an eye on you in case you headed straight into bad trouble. You see, I'm in charge of his agents along this section of the coast. We know the Nazis are just aching to get all naval movements to and from the Orkney and Shetland Islands bases. And we've caught more than one of the rats since that U-boat slipped into Scapa Flow and got the *Royal Oak.*"

"He didn't tell you what my job was?" Combat asked sharply.

"No, not a word. Naturally, I didn't ask. But why was he shot? Who shot him?"

Combat didn't reply at once. Tears were pressing against the backs of his own eyes. Had Sir John had a premonition of coming death and used his last few minutes on earth to give him what protection he could and yet not reveal the secret of

FUEHRER

his mission? It was probably true, for that was just like the aged Bureau chief. He had faith in his men and kept their secrets his secrets, but always he watched out for their welfare as much as circumstances would permit. Yes, Sir John had sent him north on a dangerous and secretive mission, but he had given Stark orders to watch over him and give him complete assistance should it be needed.

It was comforting to Combat. He and Sir John had been the only two who knew the truth, and now Sir John was dead. It was a comfort to know that Sir John had not only trusted him completely to do the job, but had made it possible for him to seek help if he needed it. And the feeling was strong in him that he would need help... Stark's help.

HE MOTIONED the C.O. to a chair, seated himself on the edge of his cot, then told the whole story from beginning to end, leaving out nothing. Stark listened silent, pop-eyed, and flabbergasted.

"God Almighty—Jackson!" he breathed when Combat finished and gave him the decoded telegram to read. "Right here in my squadron! Hell, I should go out and shoot myself. I...."

The C.O. stopped short and looked hard at Combat.

"I hate to pose as the sentimental type, Combat," he said slowly. "But the trust you show in me by telling me all this means more than I could ever tell you. I pray to God I'll some day have the chance to show you what it means. You didn't have to, you know."

"I know," Combat smiled and grasped the hand that was stretched out to him. "But... well, I want to smash this thing for Sir John if it's the last thing I do. And finding out what you thought of him, too, sort of made me want your help. After all, if one of us should fail, there's always the other to carry on. But, as a result of your work up here, can you give me any pieces to fit into the puzzle?"

"Not a thing, not a damn thing," Stark said unhappily. "I don't even know the code that this Thirty-Six used in the telegram. Of course the 'Gallant' is one of the mine trawlers anchored off Wick, but dammit, that's an English boat. Been here for weeks. The rowboats, of course, are down on the beach. The trawler crews use them for coming ashore, and there's a few the local fishermen use. But anything else? I didn't even know poor old Roberts was working up around here. Knew him quite well. Damn stout fellow. One of the best."

If Combat was disappointed at receiving no new parts for the puzzle from Major Stark, he at least didn't let it show on his face.

"Think it's okay for me to start solo patrol work tomorrow?" he asked. Then with a glance at the window, "Today, I mean."

"No reason why not," Stark replied. "Some brass hats are flying up for a routine inspection, but I don't expect they'll be here long. But Combat, you're sitting right on a keg of powder with no idea who might touch it off at any minute. I mean, this Thirty-Six is sure to learn about Jackson. In fact, he may possibly know that you're here right now. What do you plan to do about that?"

Combat scowled at the floor for a couple of moments. He had thought more than a little about that possibility himself, and had come to no definite decision. As a thought came to him he glanced up at Stark.

"That radiogram about Jackson," he said. "Did it mention he'd been in a scrap?"

"It did," Stark nodded. "But I put two and two together, and decided to make it a crash to the others—at least, until I'd had a talk with you. But it floored me, I can tell you!"

"I imagine," Combat grinned. Then, with a frown, "But what about the radio man who received the message?"

"One of *my* men, don't worry," Stark said. "But what are you driving at?"

"A hope that Thirty-Six, or any of his crew of rats, don't find out about it for a day or so," Combat said and tapped the telegram. "But I've got to chance it. I might scout the Forsinard section for days and not spot anything. But this trawler 'Gallant' ties in somewhere. I've got to chance it that this Thirty-Six—God, do I hope I meet him some day—doesn't learn about Jackson until I contact the 'Gallant'."

"And that is nothing but a slim hope," Stark grunted. "You haven't any idea what to look for, what to expect."

Combat stared hard at the telegram, then grunted. "The hell I haven't!" he said tight lipped. "*Trouble!* But blast their lousy hides, let them sling all of it my way they want. I'll be ready for them—I hope!"

"And so do I!" Major Stark echoed fervently.

CHAPTER 8
LIGHTS OUT!

BY MID-AFTERNOON that next day, Combat realized only too well how correct had been his remark to Major Stark that he might scout the Forsinard section for days and not spot anything. Since dawn he had made four solo patrols over the area and on each of them he had spotted nothing. Nothing—and yet perhaps a hundred different spots in the rugged mountainous terrain where Varden Frankle's prison and Formula Q "plant" *might* be located. And that was the maddening thought that plagued him as he eased down for his fourth landing on Fifty-Nine's field—the very probable possibility that he had actually flown over the spot and not known it. As he thought back to his talk with Sir John, a dry smile twisted his lips. He had suggested to the Bureau chief that the quickest way to get results was to *comb* the area? Hells bells, it would require the services of the entire British Army to check on everything in that wilderness section. It made him feel like hell to admit it to himself; but he was firmly convinced that he'd never in this world search out the missing chemist's prison this way.

"It's a waste of time," he said grimly and taxied up to the hangar line. "And besides, repeated patrols over that section will arouse the suspicions of the rats who must be keeping a watch. Nope, the patrol stuff is out. My only hope is that I'll get a tiny break tonight, at midnight. I'll keep my fingers crossed."

With a silent fervent prayer to echo the thought, he cut the switch and throttle and legged out. The corporal mechanic who took charge of his plane shot him a questioning look. He grinned and shook his head.

"Hunting no good," he said. "Gas her up. I may take another try at spotting a U-boat later."

The mechanic grinned and got right to work at once. He had considered it an honor to be put in charge of the ship of a pilot who had nailed a German plane before he even reported to the squadron for duty. It gave him something to boast about in the non-coms' mess. He could boast even more if his pilot repeated again—and again. Sure, it might even get him a sergeant's stripes in time.

And so he pitched into his job with a happy heart and high hopes for his pilot's next patrol.

Oblivious to his mechanic's thoughts, Combat went over to the mess and got a drink at the bar.

A few minutes later Stark came in and joined him.

"Spot anything, Cramer?" the C.O. asked for the benefit of the three or four other pilots in the mess.

"Nothing, sir," Combat said and gave Stark a meaning look. "Not a damn U-boat, but there could have been a million of them down there and I wouldn't spot them in a month of Sundays."

"Tough, too bad," Stark murmured as the light of hope in his eyes died. "Well, perhaps...."

He stopped short and cocked an ear. So did everybody else. From outside came the sound of a twin-engined job coming down to a landing. Major Stark sighed and hastily finished his drink.

"The inspection party from Air Ministry," he grunted. "Why don't they leave us alone?"

"They have to do something to hold their rank," Combat murmured. "Do you expect them to stay long?"

"No," Stark replied. Then, with a quick look at Combat. "No, they'll be gone before evening."

They all trooped outside to watch the huge Vickers Wellington bomber settle to earth and come trundling into the line. A general and two colonels climbed down out of the cabin, and when Combat saw them he started violently.

"Damn!" he muttered. "Why does everything happen to me?"

He was standing apart from the others with Major Stark. The C.O. heard his remark and shot an inquiring look at him.

"What now?" he asked.

"Might just as well have published it in the *Times* I was

coming up here," Combat said. "General Doaks, of Staff. Colonel Wilson, his aide. And Colonel Preston, head of Air Ministry

Personnel Bureau. I've met all three. They've met me. See what I mean? You can't present me as Lieutenant Cramer."

"Duck out of sight, and stay there," Stark said. "Then I won't have to present you at all."

"Good idea," Combat nodded and turned away. "See you later."

THEN BEGAN four solid hours of playing hide and seek with three Air Ministry high rankers. The visitors took a look at everything, save perhaps the insides of the engines in the ships, and all the while Combat was several steps ahead of them and ducking into some other building to hide until they passed on by. And then when it seemed as though he had won, fate kicked over the apple cart. He had slipped into C Flight hangar to watch the take-off when who should come strolling into that hangar but the three gentlemen in person. It was too late to duck out. General Doaks spotted him.

"I say, Captain Combat!" the stiff-shirted high ranker boomed. "You attached to this squadron, eh?"

A mechanic standing at rigid attention almost toppled over and Combat would gladly have given five years of his life to have pasted General Doaks right smack on the nose. However, the damage had been done and he was strictly behind the eight ball. He forced a smile to his lips, saluted, and then stepped forward to shake hands with all three of them. They talked for a few minutes and Combat lied as well as he could. He was tempted to ask them not to say who he was, and explain that he was on a special assignment under the name of Cramer. However, the mechanic still standing a few yards away killed the idea deader than a doornail.

Finally, the trio shook hands with him again and started to take their departure. Colonel Wilson was the last to shake his hand, and the man's sharp blue eyes looked straight into his as he smiled.

"Glad to have seen you again, Combat," he said. "And good luck!"

"Thank you, Colonel," Combat said. And when he saw the tight smile on the lips of both General Doaks and Colonel Preston, he was almost egged into adding, "Well, why in hell don't all three of you blab to this greaseball that I'm working on some Intelligence job?"

He didn't say it, of course, but when the three were in the Wellington and the big ship was roaring across the field, he walked over to the mechanic and took a steel fingered grip on the man's arm.

"Were you ever in the prize ring?" he asked in a hard voice.

The greaseball blinked stupidly. "Why, no, sir!" he gulped. "Why, sir?"

"I wanted to know," Combat said and tightened his grip, "if *you* knew what it felt like to be cut to ribbons and knocked right into the hospital for a couple of weeks!"

"No, sir," the mechanic said and winced from the grip on his arm. "I can't say that I do, sir."

"It's not nice," Combat said. "Hurts worse than a bullet in the belly. Forget these last five minutes. I'm Lieutenant Cramer. Got that all clear?"

"Yes, sir!" the other gulped. "Perfectly! I understand, Lieutenant."

"So help me, you'd better," the Yank ace said grimly. "If any of the other mechanics…."

"They won't, sir!"

"See that they don't!" Combat clipped.

EXACTLY SIX hours later he was walking across the drome in the darkness toward the small waterfront fishing village of Wick. Hope was burning fiercely in him, but it was being tormented by a thousand and one conflicting thoughts. Many times had he bucked against the blank wall of war's intrigue, and eventually smashed his way through into the light beyond. Yet, on every other occasion he had been armed. No, not armed with things that spit out bullets and death; armed with at least one concrete fact upon which he could plan and build his next step.

This time, though, there was nothing. His enemies held every single one of the cards. He knew not one definite thing about them, and they knew *everything* about him. God, it was like making a night scouting patrol through No Man's Land with a glowing flashlight in both hands. He was headed for the third rowboat from the left of the row down there on the beach. He'd seen it at least fifty times during the day. And he was going to row out toward the British mine trawler 'Gallant,' anchored off shore. He'd even seen her come in that evening with the rest of the fleet from their daily task of sweeping up any mines U-boats might have laid during the dark hours of the night. The 'Gallant' was his only hope.

He swung his head around, trying to spot any silhouette of

a man against the dull glow of the hangar lights. But he was sure that nobody was tailing him. That didn't relieve his mind, however, as he moved onward. A picture of the face of that mechanic standing at rigid attention in the hangar kept coming back to him. Of course he had told Stark of the episode, but the C.O. had vouched for the grease-ball to the limit. His name was Brewster, and he had served with Stark long before war had broken out. No, Stark would stake anything on Brewster keeping his mouth shut.

Thoughts of that hangar affair still prickled Combat, and when he finally reached the third boat in the row, beads of nervous sweat were soaking into his undershirt. When he started to push the boat out into deep water he was suddenly filled with the urge to call all bets off; to tackle the job from some different angle. However, one unanswerable question stopped him from doing that, and made him get into the boat and pick up the sculling oar. It was simply… what other angle could he select? None!

Sticking grimly to his purpose, he eased away from the shore and headed across the dark waters toward the faintly glowing mast light of the trawler 'Gallant.' The sculling lock was well greased, and the only sound made was the soft swish of the oar feathering through the water, but to Combat's tight nerves it had all the earmarks of a bracket barrage before zero hour. With every passing second he expected to be challenged by some trawler seaman standing watch. But when he was a good quarter of a mile off shore he realized that the trawler men used those boats to and from shore, and if he was seen he would undoubtedly be taken for one of them.

HE FELT a little better after that and increased his stroke. Finally he reached the 'Gallant' and was in close under her lee. He rested his oar and used his hands to fend off the bow. And meanwhile he stared up at the line the deck rail made against the sky and waited. Wait was the only thing he could do. If he was expected somebody would be on the watch for him. And if he wasn't—if the 'Gallant' truly was all English, from crew to rudder post—then there was no use making his presence known.

However, as the seconds mounted up to total perhaps three minutes, he strangely enough began to believe that the 'Gallant' really did mean something. He did for the reason that there must be a watch aboard, and the watch would have seen him sliding up alongside the ship. And that watch, if English, would certainly challenge him. Yet, why didn't somebody come to the ship's side? He couldn't stay there and fend off all night!

Hopes, fears, and dreads ran rampant through him, and then suddenly his aching eyes saw the silhouetted head and shoulders leaning over the rail.

"Give it!" came the whispered demand.

For a split second Combat didn't get it, then it came to him in a flash.

"Three cheers," he whispered back the countersign.

The head and shoulders ducked out of sight and were gone a couple of minutes. Then they reappeared and one end of a rope ladder hit Combat lightly on the face. He caught hold of it, steadied himself for a second, and then went cat-like up and over the side.

He was led through three separate curtains hung in the companionway to block off all light from inside, and on into what appeared to be the skipper's quarters. Three men sat at a table bolted to the floor. They all wore rough, deep sea clothing, but on each man's cap was the gold braid insignia of Royal Navy Reserve—the honor rank given to British fishermen who volunteered for mine sweeping duty.

An empty feeling spread through Combat's stomach as he stared into those three sets of cold, hostile eyes. Then the man who sat in the middle spoke.

"The countersign?" he demanded.

Combat gave it and didn't miss the shadow that passed over the trawler captain's eyes for a moment. The man seemed confused, undecided. Combat suddenly felt as though he were standing right on the lip of a huge bottomless pit. In sheer desperation he took a long shot in the dark. He pulled out the coded telegram and tossed it on the table.

"I obey Thirty-Six's orders," he said. "There they are."

The captain read the telegram and looked relieved.

"You are a new one, eh?" he grunted. "But that is Thirty-Six's business, of course. He must not have told you about the second countersign we hide in the rowboat, in case the swine British discover the first one. Well, never mind. I have your instructions. They are from Berlin. You are to land on Murdock's farm and contact Agent Four. Tell him that...."

The cabin door opening cut off the rest of the captain's words.

He swung around in his chair, a snarl twisting his lips. The snarl faded as the seaman who entered handed him a slip of paper. He grunted as he read it, scowled at the ceiling, and tapped the slip of paper on the palm of his other hand. Then he motioned to Combat's seaman escort and gave him the paper.

"You take care of this!" he growled.

The seaman read it, and started to leave the cabin. Whether he actually left, Combat didn't know, because a split second later the whole ship seemed to explode in his face: There was a tremendous blow on the back of his head, and he went sailing way out into a huge void of slowly diminishing sound!

CHAPTER 9
THE WEB OF DOOM

THE ALL-WHITE Junkers plane that *Herr* Gruber used, when there was absolutely no danger of meeting Allied airmen slid down through the night sky to land on a spot of ground far behind the Nazi Westwall known as Zone K. The plot upon which the plane came to rest had once been the well groomed polo field adjoining a now deserted château, and no sooner had the prop stopped spinning than a score of flunkies rushed over to bow and scrape before Gruber as he alighted. He ignored them all save one, a thin German infantry captain with a face like the underside of a trolley car. To him the German Leader gave an angry stare.

"He has not arrived?" he barked.

The captain shook his head, then seemed to bow it in a gesture of personal shame.

"Perhaps the weather, my *Fuehrer,*" he began. "It is perhaps bad over the Channel, and…."

The captain stopped short, and relief flooded his ugly face. He raised one hand toward the night heavens.

"A plane!" he cried. "It should be he!"

The sound of the diving plane grew louder. Gruber licked his lips in a frightened gesture and glanced hastily about as though seeking a raid shelter. Before he could make up his mind to run or stay, an English pursuit plane swooped down out of the night and landed directly alongside the white Junkers. The pilot leaped out and ran quickly over to click his heels and give Gruber the stiff-armed salute. The new arrival was Number Thirty-Six.

The German *Fuehrer* returned the salute with the usual up-flip of his clammy hand, then without a word turned on his heel and led the parade across the polo field and up into the château. Number Thirty-Six followed him silently inside and waited until Gruber had seated himself at a desk in one of the rooms that once long ago had seen fair ladies and gallant gentlemen, but now looked like most any other German military headquarters.

"It was impossible to get here sooner, *Fuehrer,*" Thirty-Six said. "But I bring you good news, however."

An eager gleam leaped into Gruber's eyes and he hitched forward in his chair so that his feet could touch the floor.

"What is the news?" he demanded. "Give me your report!"

"I have established all necessary contacts," Thirty-Six began.

"The Q bombs and guide torpedoes are all ready for transport to points of contact with the U-boats and trawlers. The destroyers to take part in the action are at their stations, and I have selected my scouting pilots and given them their instructions. There is nothing left undone that should be done."

As the man paused, Gruber scowled and drummed his fingertips on the desk.

"How about the drome your pilots will use," he said after awhile. "You are sure of complete success? There must not be any chance of failure, because that drome is the key-point of my plan. If your pilots should meet with delay our task would be more difficult. And that *must not* happen!"

Gruber shrilled the last and smashed his fist on the desk. To anyone passing by the window at that moment, it would have appeared that the German *Fuehrer* was going to throw a fit. Number Thirty-Six waited until he had calmed down, then spoke in a soothing voice.

"YOU NEED have no fears at all, *Fuehrer,*" he said. "You have said that you will strike on the ninth of April, and I promise you that on the evening of the eighth all will be in readiness for your signal. I am not one of those who would fail you. I have not failed you in the past, and I shall not fail you in the future. You have my promise on that."

"Promise?" Gruber snapped. "Bah! They mean nothing to me. However, I do admit, Number Thirty-Six, you have served me well. Continue to do so and you will not be sorry. Enough of this talk, however. I have been worried about the supplies of Formula Q. I have often wondered if we should have not brought that swine, Frankle, to Germany the very day we captured him. It might have been…."

The German leader paused and scowled at his clenched hands. Number Thirty-Six shook his head.

"It would have been impossible, *Fuehrer,*" he said. "And very dangerous to the success of our cause, too. It was best that we did what we did. As for the Formula Q supplies, there are more than enough for your needs. And… Ah, it is time for the British broadcast to the American people. I suggest you listen in. I believe you will be pleased."

Gruber grunted, got up and went over to a short-wave radio on the far wall. He turned the dial knobs, got a few seconds of screaming static, and then came the English voice speaking to listeners in the U.S.A.

This is London! The most important topic of conversation here in London tonight is a series of mysterious explosions that have taken place in and around London, and southward to the coast. Although the figure is not official, it has been stated on good authority that no less than fifty five persons have lost their lives. The explosions themselves have been very peculiar in that they have all occurred close to important points in the British system of war defense. For example, a submarine at a certain British base was blown up and sunk at her dock by a man posing as a candy peddler—yet not sixty yards away was a new ten thousand ton cruiser, and it was not touched. Experts say that the explosion which sank the submarine could very easily have put the cruiser out of commission for many weeks, if not actually sunk her.

Also, there is the case of the gale house of a munitions plant blowing up, and yet the plant itself was left untouched. Also, a river barge close to the Houses of Parliament was destroyed by a man throwing a bomb from the river bank. He had only to face the other way and he could have hurled the same bomb right through a window into the room where Parliament was holding a secret session.

Who is behind these weird bombings, everybody is asking. Well, there are two schools of thought on that subject. Some believe the Irish Republican Army is responsible, while the other group believe it is the work of German agents seeking to undermine British morale. Personally, I naturally have not formed any opinion. However, I can assure you that whether it be the I.R.A. or the Nazis, the British are going to leave no stone unturned in their concentrated efforts to track down the bombings to their source and deal accordingly with the culprits.

Now, as for the news from the Western Front. Yesterday—

Gruber snapped off the radio.

"That is fine work, Thirty-Six!" he cried. "Splendid! It will bring about just what we want, eh?"

"Without a doubt, *Fuehrer!*" the spy extraordinary nodded. "While the fools all rush around London and the southern coast seeking us, we shall be able to execute our little *Blitzkrieg* in the north without any trouble at all. Before they realize what has happened it will be too late."

"Ja, ja!" Gruber shouted and shook his fist above his head. "And the ninth of April will go down as one of the most glorious days in German history!"

"And now I should like to speak of something else, *Fueh-*

rer," Thirty-Six, said when Gruber stopped shaking his fist and beating his breast.

"Of course, of course!" *Der Fuehrer* said. "Go ahead. What is it you wish to tell me now?"

Thirty-Six hesitated, and a thin smile tightened his lips.

"IT IS something which should answer your question

PEIPLOW

completely as to whether we have sufficient supplies of Formula Q," he said. "Right now there is a British cruiser of the Duchess class riding at anchor a few miles off Kinnaird's Head, on the Northeast coast of Scotland. I know she will be there for the next twenty-hours at least, because repairs are being made to one of her screws. I also have a complete plan of the mine field behind which she believes she's protected."

"Yes, yes, what about her?" Gruber demanded impatiently, as the other paused for breath.

"This, *Fuehrer,*" Thirty-Six said. "Our light cruiser, *Hesse,* is almost an exact copy of the Duchess class of British cruiser, as you well know. You also know that it is now in the North Sea, working with the U-boat flotilla. She can be reached by plane in a few hours. And she was one of the first ships to be fitted with Q bombs and guide torpedoes. Run up the British ensign on her and she could steam right up to the British coast and not be challenged."

"Ah!" Gruber breathed softly. "I begin to see what you mean. The *Hesse* will steam up and destroy the English cruiser, yes?"

"Exactly!" Thirty-Six nodded. "The *Hesse* will circle her with her guide torpedo, and that will be the end of her. Now, would not that be proof to you if you saw it with your own eyes, my *Fuehrer?*"

Gruber blinked, and gulped slightly. "You suggest I should make the trip aboard the *Hesse*, and observe?"

"But of course!" Thirty-Six cried. "It would not only be a wonderful thing for you to see, but it would be an honor for the officers and crew of the *Hesse*. They would tell the whole Reich of how you, their *Fuehrer*, were there."

"Yes, yes, that is so," the German leader murmured as his face turned just a shade paler. "But I doubt I could spare the time."

"But there would be something else for you to see!" Thirty-Six spoke up quickly. "Something that I have saved for you alone. The death of the one you hate most. Captain Combat!"

"Combat?" Gruber shrilled, and came right up out of his chair. "That *Schweinehund?* Where is he? Have you captured him yet? I meant to ask you about that dog sooner. You swore to kill him, you know."

"And I shall," Thirty-Six said assuringly. "Where he is at this very moment, I do not know. But I have a pretty good idea.

However, he will be in our hands in plenty of time. Yes, he will be our swine guest of honor aboard the *Hesse.*"

"It will give me great pleasure to kill him with my own hands!" Gruber snarled.

"I agree," Thirty-Six nodded. "But I believe I have a way that we will both enjoy much more. It is this, my *Fuehrer.*"

The spy leaned forward and spoke for a couple of minutes and drew word pictures with gestures of his two hands. When he was finished his face was beet red from the sense of savage accomplishment that burned within him. Gruber's face had turned a muddy sort of orange, but his eyes gleamed with wild, excited triumph.

"That is perfect, perfect!" he hissed. "I congratulate you again for thinking of such a wonderful idea!"

"I was sure you would think so!" Thirty-Six beamed. "It will be a marvelous sight, and one which you will long remember."

Der Fuehrer blinked again and swallowed. In the excitement of learning of how his most hated enemy would die, he had momentarily forgotten that to witness the deed would necessitate his leaving the protection of his Nazi den. However, he had walked into his own trap and he did not dare to back out. His hold on the German populace was not quite what he would like it to be... or what it would be a year from then, he hoped!

"Yes, it will be wonderful," he said with an effort. "And I shall watch it, myself. We will leave for Kiel at once. Congratulations, again, Thirty-Six! Yes, I have a feeling that you will go far in my service."

CHAPTER 10
THE HELL SHIP

W HEN CONSCIOUSNESS returned to Bill Combat it brought back with it the crazy impression that he was being repeatedly tossed up and down in a soaking wet blanket, and that each time he came down, water was splashed on his face and a revolver was fired off in his brain. Then gradually he realized that his eyes were open. Directly above him was a spread of fog or smoke that rushed down toward him one moment, and retreated the next. And all the while, the revolver kept banging away inside his head.

In time though, when his head cleared and the revolver reports were less sharp, memory came sneaking back to him. He had been clouted on the head in the captain's cabin aboard the trawler 'Gallant.' And now he was flat on the deck of a boat that was hammering through choppy seas under a thin blanket of fog. Somewhere off to his right it was lighter. He figured it to be the morning sun coming up over the fog. He tried to push up to a sitting position to make sure, but the effort was too much for him. He fell back gasping and his head cracked the deck and seemed to split into two separate pieces and roll away from his shoulders in opposite directions.

A harsh laugh to his left drove the pain fog from his brain and eyes and forced him to turn his head. Sitting comfortably on a coil of mooring hawser was the captain of the 'Gallant.' So he was *still* on the 'Gallant,' eh? And it was pounding out to sea, for he realized that the throbbing in his head was partly from the beat of the engines below decks. He tried again to lift himself up to a sitting position and was just able to make it. As it was, he was forced to close his eyes tight and fight hard to stop his stomach from coming right up through his front teeth.

The trawler captain laughed again and leaned forward, letting the Luger he held dangle over one crossed knee.

"So the great Captain Combat got hurt, eh?" he said grinning. "And he didn't like it at all? Now, that is too bad!"

His bellow of delight drowned out the thump of the engines and the whistle of the wind in the rigging. Combat made no comment. He was feeling too awful to care, even if the captain laughed himself to death. He concentrated on getting himself under control. Now that his head wasn't against the deck, the throbbing ceased considerably and began to gradually fade away. However, he was plenty weak around the edges, and in an abstract way he was sort of glad of that. If he'd felt his old self, he would have come up off that deck and climbed the captain like a pole, and to hell with the Luger in his hand.

Perhaps, though, his sub-conscious mind caused him to make a move in that direction, because a gleam leaped into the trawler captain's eyes and his Luger jerked up from its dangling position.

"Come ahead!" the man jeered. "*Himmel*, yes! It is a bit chilly, and a bit of exercise will warm me up. Nor will I kill you, either. I couldn't do that. I'm supposed to save you for Thirty-Six!"

"*Thirty-Six?*" Combat echoed before he could stop himself.

The trawler captain slapped his knee and looked confounded.

"Why, didn't you know?" he cried. Then, "But, of course not. I didn't give you a chance to read that radiogram, did I? Just had my seaman put you to sleep and save me the bother. Well, it was from Thirty-Six, saying that you might come aboard, and if you did to keep you all safe and sound for him."

Combat said nothing. He sat staring out across the fog-topped waves. He saw a couple of other trawlers, but their presence didn't register on his brain. It was too filled with the bitter realization that he had walked headlong into a trap. He had done just what his enemy had figured he would do. Yet, how did Thirty-Six know he was at Fifty-Nine? How did Thirty-Six know he had obtained that coded telegram off Jackson's dead body? And how did Thirty-Six know that he had taken the rowboat and gone out to the trawler?

THE NAME of Major Stark flashed across his brain, and for one agonizing second he felt doubt. In the next second, though, he was ashamed of his thought. Stark wasn't Thirty-Six. He just *couldn't* be! Hell, was it Brewster, the mechanic? Combat thought of the man and his hands unconsciously closed into rock-hard fists.

The trawler captain saw the impulsive movement and laughed.

"It's a shame, isn't it?" the man jeered. "There you thought you were going to trip us all up very neatly, and see what happened to you? Well, I've heard tell a lot of you, but now that I meet you I'm sort of disappointed. Any man in my crew is better than you. We're clever, we are!"

"Think of that the day the British navy catches up with you!" Combat grated. Then, moving his hand slightly. "Those other trawlers manned by some of your own breed?"

The captain snorted and spat on the deck.

"Them?" he grunted. "No, they're fools that are willing to risk their bloody necks for a couple of shillings from the King. They make me sick, the lot of them. Me, I get paid good money when I risk my neck. And you can take that for the bloody truth, Mister Captain Combat."

What anger the Yank held for the man faded away at his words. It became loathing instead. A loathing for something lower than a man and lower than an animal. Even the most vicious and deadly of animals had their own code. But there was no code among the breed of rats aboard the 'Gallant.' God, King, Country meant nothing to them. They were world wanderers, wharf rats. Cross their palms with enough silver and they'd slit the throats of their own parents. Their breed had polluted the last war, they were polluting this one.

"Mind telling me where we're headed?" Combat asked, as though speaking would cleanse the taste of the other's words from his mouth.

"Sure," the captain said, and pointed a finger toward the bow. "Out there aways. Weren't thinking of asking me to turn back, were you?"

The man boomed out some more laughter, and for the hundredth time Combat gauged the distance between them. And for the hundredth time he gave up the idea. After all, there were others besides the belly-shaking captain aboard. And going over the side wouldn't be any better than staying aboard. His fate was in the lap of time, and so for the present....

He let the rest slide by the boards, as at that moment there came to him a sound that made his heart turn over. It was the sound of airplane engines up in the fog, or above it. And if he knew his airplane sounds, those were Supermarine Spitfires up there. Impulsively he started up on his feet. The trawler captain moved like a striking cobra. A fist drove deep into Combat's stomach, and the Luger barrel was dragged down his left cheek.

"No funny business!" the trawler captain snarled.

Combat tried frantically to lash out with just one fist. His brain was on fire with rage, and all sound reasoning had fled him for the second. However, he might just as well have tried to pull down the trawler's stack and belted the captain with it. White fire filled his belly, his eyes were blurred, and his brain spinning. He fell down onto the deck and lay there, grimly fighting back the surging wave of oblivion.

"Mate, come here!" the captain bellowed.

Feet pounded along the deck and stopped.

"Aye, sir?"

"Carry the scum into the cabin and tie him up!" the captain ordered. "He's hearing the sound of some of his pals up there in the fog. We'll be running out of the stuff soon, and I don't want him sleeping around on the deck. Tie him up good. I'm going forward to tend to the radio business. Anything come through yet?"

"Nothing we need worry about, Skipper," the owner of the feet replied. Then with a chuckle, "If he shouldn't want me to tie him up, what should I do, huh?"

"Hit him with that feather duster again!" the captain cried, and walked off roaring with laughter.

The urge to fight lashed through Combat, and his brain

screamed to his muscles for action. However, though the spirit was strong the battered flesh was weak. The seaman, the same seaman who had met him at the Gallant's lee rail last night, took a length of stout cord from his pocket, jerked Combat's arms behind his back and lashed them tight. Then, stepping back, he kicked the Yank in the ribs.

"Get up, you swine!" he snarled. "Think I'm going to carry your blinking hide in my two hands? Get up, I say!" Combat felt the man's booted toe four times before he could manage to struggle up on his feet. Even then he almost didn't make it. He swayed like a stalk of wheat in the wind, but cold spray slapping over the rail was good on his face and helped him to stay upright. The seaman gave him a shove forward.

"Get along to the Skipper's quarters!" the man growled. "And if you fall down you'll feel my boot some more. Get on with you!"

Teeth clenched tight, the Yank stumbled aft and in through the triple curtained entrance to the captain's quarters. Once they were inside, the seaman spun him around and then gave him a push that spilled him back helpless in a chair. Combat choked back the groan of pain that rose up to his lips.

"You wouldn't mind telling me your name, would you?" he asked.

The seaman stared dumbly at him for a moment and then chuckled.

"And why not?" he grunted. "It's Griggs. Jackie Griggs, that's what it is. And you can find it on the Port Captain's Register at Wick, if you've a mind to look it up. But you'll not be having the chance to do that."

"Why not?" Combat asked the man casually.

"He asks why not?" the seaman echoed to an imaginary third person in the cabin. "The swine bloke thinks maybe he'll live to tell the truth about this little tub, and them that mans her. Or wasn't you thinking of that, eh?"

The seaman stuck his face forward and laughed as he spoke the last. Combat shrugged. "Maybe I was," he said. "But I wanted to know your name for a very different reason."

The not very bright seaman blinked and fastened suspicious eyes on Combat. "Is that so, huh?" he grunted. "What's the reason?"

"I want to know how to address you when I return all the little compliments you've given me," Combat said.

"Compliments?" the other growled frowning. "What kind?"

"A crack on the head," Combat said. "And a few kicks in the ribs, and so forth."

The seaman didn't get it for a second. When he did, his eyes narrowed and his face darkened up like a thunderhead. Combat didn't even have time to regret speaking so spontaneously. A juggernaut roared up out of somewhere and practically caved in the side of his head. He went flying out of the chair and down onto the floor.

HE LAY there as colored balls of light whirled and spun around before his eyes, and the trawler's screw seemed to chew its three-bladed way right through his head. After awhile he heard the snarling voice of the trawler's captain. The man was in a terrific fury, but this time his fury was directed at somebody else, not Combat.

"You dumb-headed waterfront scum!" the captain cursed. "I said you could tap him a couple if you want to. But I didn't say to break his damn head. By God, if he dies you'll wish you was never born!"

"But the bloke made me mad!" came the protesting voice of the seaman.

The string of salt water curses that poured from the captain's mouth must have blistered the paint clear down below the waterline to the keel.

"And what do you think Thirty-Six will be, if this swine dies?" he finished up in a thunder of sound. "He'll have you cut in pieces one by one and tossed to the fishes. And me too, most likely. More of that sea water! We got to bring him to, if possible. We'll be making contact most any minute, now."

More curses spilled from the captain's mouth, but Combat didn't hear them all. He didn't because they were cut off by half of the North Sea splashing down over him. Even if he wanted to play dead dog he wouldn't have had a chance. That icy sea water would have made an Egyptian mummy stir. He groaned and spluttered in spite of himself, and his eyes flew open. The anger and worry stamped on the face of the Gallant's captain staring down at him faded away and became inexpressible relief instead. The captain reached down, caught hold of his shoulder and pulled him up to a sitting position. With his other hand he scooped up a mug of ship's grog and held it to Combat's lips.

"Drink it, and not too fast!" he ordered.

It would have been cutting off his own nose to spite his face had Combat refused. Besides, he needed that grog damn bad, so he drank it right down to the last drop. The powerful liquid burned straight down to the bottom of his shoes, but it stayed down there, and when finally he got his breath back his head felt more like one piece again, and his red, filmed eyes cleared considerably.

It was then, as he looked around, that he realized he must have been out cold, or at least semi-unconscious, for a considerable length of time. He was out on the deck again, sitting beside the port scuppers, about amidships. The fog was gone though the sun was stilled dulled by a high altitude strata of cloud scud. Also, the 'Gallant' was plowing along all by herself. There was no sign of the rest of the trawler fleet. The 'Gallant's' captain seemed to read his thoughts.

"We just lost them in the fog," he said and laughed. "But I'll bet we make port afore they do, at that. Now, up on your feet and we'll walk about a bit. You got to look nice when you meet Thirty-Six, you know."

As the captain heaved him up on his feet, Combat grinned though it was an effort.

"It's how I'll act, you should worry about," he said. "I don't think this Thirty-Six will like it if I collapse at his feet from the beating I've received. By the way, who is he?"

"Ask him, if you can tell which is him!" the captain snapped. "And I'm not worrying about you collapsing, either. You put up quite a fight before we could capture you, you know."

COMBAT WAS quite willing for the captain to walk him up and down the slightly heaving deck. His legs were very rubbery, and exercise would stiffen them up a bit. It would also clear his head more. If he wanted to stand any chance at all against what was to come—whatever it was—he at least had to get himself into as good shape as possible. Then, too, there was another reason why a walk up and down the deck was all right with him.

He had noticed a pile of boxes forward near the bow. They were small, about six inches square and six inches deep. Felt pads were fastened about each individual box, and the whole lot—they took up perhaps two cubic yards of space—was enveloped by a sling net and fastened securely to the deck. What they were or what they contained, he had no idea. However, their presence aboard a mine sweeper looked very much out of place.

When the captain started to turn him around and away from them, he held back and nodded his head.

"Lunch boxes for the crew?" he asked in an innocent tone.

The captain glanced at the pile, then favored him with a wide evil grin.

"Yeah!" he chuckled. "For British crews when they get down to Davy Jones' Locker. Why, even you might be given one of them, but that's up to Thirty-Six. He's in charge of the Q business, and…."

The captain gulped and snapped his lips shut, and the knowledge of having said too much pushed the color up into his face. He angrily swung Combat around and started him back along the deck. The Yank walked along like a man in a dream. However he was far from dreaming.

Those boxes contained Formula Q explosives! Formula Q—destined for German U-boats and other war craft at sea? He imagined so, and he'd probably find out before his voyage aboard the Gallant was at an end. But there was one thing he *had* found out. Supplies of Formula Q smuggled out of England were smuggled out by the trawler 'Gallant.' Perhaps, then, by other trawlers manned by German money-killers who posed as British fishermen risking their lives to do their bit for England.

Then suddenly, as a bit of forgotten memory came rushing back into Yank's brain, he almost stumbled and lost step with his escort. It was memories of words spoken just before that radio man had entered the captain's cabin. The captain had started to give him instructions, believing him to be one of Thirty-Six's men. And he had said:

"You are to land on Murdock's farm and contact Agent Four."

MURDOCK'S FARM! That must be the place where Varden Frankle was being kept a prisoner… if Frankle actually was alive. But it was undoubtedly the plant where Formula Q was being made. Murdock's farm! If there was a Murdock's farm in the Forsinard section, then one single sentence spoken by the captain of the 'Gallant' had gained him more than all his other efforts.

"Yeah, Murdock's farm!" he said to himself. "But will you ever live to smoke it out? You've got to, kid. You've got to. Here you are out on the North Sea and heading straight for a nasty end, if the signs mean anything. But you've been headed toward a nasty end a couple of other times in your war career, and didn't make contact. Lady Luck, make it unanimous, old gal!"

Breathing that prayer over and over again to himself, Combat let the captain walk him up and down until a sharp cry carried down from the lookout in the crow's nest.

"Cruiser off the port bow!"

The trawler's captain stopped short, then, practically hurling Combat into a seaman's arms, he hurried forward to the bridge. Combat peered hard ahead and to port. At first, all he could see was a faint blurred line down on the horizon. But as it grew larger and larger and began to take shape, he could see the outline of a cruiser pounding down the sea toward the trawler under a full head of steam. And a few minutes later his heart almost leaped out of his chest as he saw the British ensign flying at the masthead.

In that moment of intense excitement a moth-eaten old saying from "meller-drama" days flashed through his head and he spoke it aloud.

"Boom, boom!" 'Tis the Battleship Oregon! Boys, we are saved!"

The seaman stared at him opened-mouth, then burst into a roar of laughter.

"So the crack on your head has knocked you off your beam, eh?" he hooted. "The Battleship Oregon, huh? You blinky scum, what would the American Navy be doing over here? And don't worry, it ain't!"

It was then Combat suddenly realized that he was the only person aboard the 'Gallant' who seemed excited about the approach of the British cruiser. And when no attempt was made to shove him down below decks out of sight, a queer feeling stole through his stomach. Why were they letting him remain on deck? That was a British cruiser, right enough, of the Duchess class; he recognized the lines. And the Union Jack was flying.

Desperately trying to figure the answers and not even coming close to first base, he watched the cruiser bear down on them and then heave to—to windward. The trawler's engines eased off and she was nosed in close, but not too close. And preparations were made to lower two of the 'Gallant's' boats. Tearing his eyes from the boat-lowering proceedings Combat raked the decks of the sleek cruiser with a glance. Men in Jack Tar suits swarmed over the deck like ants under the barking orders of junior naval officers.

And then, as Combat raised his eyes to the quarterdeck, he received a stunning blow. There were five high-ranking navy officers standing there on the quarterdeck, and one man in military uniform. All of the uniforms were German, and the one in military garb was *Herr* Gruber.

"Gruber!" Combat gasped. *"Der Fuehrer* and five German navy men aboard a British cruiser?"

"Yeah!" he heard the seaman at his side. "A British cruiser— only she ain't. She's German, and a bloody fine ship she is, too!"

CHAPTER 11
VENGEANCE AT SEA!

THE EVENTS of the next fifteen minutes of Bill Combat's life were like those of a mad, crazy nightmare, and a hundred times he unconsciously told himself that such was the case; that he was having a bad spell of dreams and would wake up to reality very shortly.

He did wake up to reality, and also to the fact that it was no nightmare. The supposedly British cruiser was under the command of Nazi naval officers. And no less than *Herr* Gruber was with them. Into one of the trawler's boats the boxes of Formula Q were gently placed as though they were so many newborn babes. A couple of the trawler's men took the boat across the narrow strip of water to the cruiser, and the "touchy" cargo was lifted up on board.

Into the second trawler boat Combat was dumped, with little ceremony. The captain leaned over the rail and shouted parting jibes at him, but Combat paid no attention. As soon as he was settled in the boat he returned his gaze to the five uniformed figures on the cruiser's quarterdeck. The group passed from his view as the rowboat came alongside the boarding ladder. His escort seaman practically hauled him up onto the cruiser's deck, let go of him and saluted the deck officer.

"Captain's compliments, and here is the prisoner," he said, in low caste German.

The deck officer nodded and made a motion with his hand. "Very well," he said. "Return to your boat."

The seaman paused long enough to leer at Combat and lick his lips, then he turned toward the opening in the rail to go down the boarding ladder. There was much that the Yank would have loved to be able to do at the moment, but couldn't because his arms were still lashed behind his back. His feet and legs were free, however, and in the second or so allowed he made full use of them. As the seaman bent over to grasp the ladder, Combat turned quickly and brought up his right foot with all the driving power of a man trying a field goal from the fifty-five yard line. His boot caught the seaman right flush on the spot he aimed

93

at. A wild bellow of alarm burst from the seaman's mouth, and he grabbed frantically for a hold on something and missed. His body curved outward and down like an exhibition high diver. His head cracked against the gunwale of the boat below, and he bounced off into the water.

The men on the deck of the cruiser stood stunned and dumbfounded for a moment, then they leaped upon Combat as though he were some captured animal who had broken through the bars of his cage! They threw him down onto the deck, but the jarring throbs in his head were nothing to the sense of satisfaction that surged through him. When the others realized he was making no attempt to give battle they pulled him up on his feet again and looked at the deck officer for instructions. They came from the quarterdeck.

"Bring the prisoner up here!"

A few moments later Combat stood facing the group he had seen first from the deck of the trawler. It was then he recognized one of the men in navy uniform as Hermann Peiplow, chief of German Intelligence. He stood beside Gruber, and the triumphant blaze in his eyes was equal to that in the *Fuehrer's*. The three other naval officers were faintly familiar to Combat from pictures he had seen in the papers. One of them, however, garbed as a lieutenant commander, struck a particularly familiar note in Combat's memory. He felt sure he had met the man before, and in the flesh, not in some newspaper picture.

THE MAN was fairly tall; he had a high forehead, a sharp face, and a thick mustache that hid most of his mouth. Part of that mouth he could see was stretched back in a pleased smile.

And as Combat looked into the pale eyes he saw the glint of smug, dancing delight. Then suddenly, Combat knew! There was not one trace of proof on which to base his certain belief. Something just naturally seemed to click in his brain and tell him that the man was Number Thirty-Six. The fact that he'd actually met the man before became more and more pronounced in him. But when, where, and under what circumstances, he could not for the life of him remember.

But he was positive that the mysterious Number Thirty-Six stood there before him. He forced a grin to his lips and looked straight into the pale eyes.

"Fancy meeting you here, Thirty-Six!" he said in a casual voice.

The lieutenant commander started violently and his eyes bugged out for a second. Then he got control of himself, and broadened his smile. "I arranged it," he said. "So it is no surprise to me. But, suppose I am not this Thirty-Six, eh?"

"Then that would make you a liar," Combat grinned at him. "But you can clear up a point, if you would? Where was the last time we met? It skips me for the moment."

Combat wasn't sure, but he thought he saw a look of marked relief flash across the other's face. He redoubled his efforts to pin down the facts regarding a previous meeting with the man, but it was all just vague nothingness in his brain. At that moment Gruber refused to play second fiddle any longer.

"It doesn't matter!" he snapped. "You will never be seeing him again, anyway. You're going to die!"

Combat looked into the blazing eyes then turned puzzled eyes back to Thirty-Six.

"Who's this guy?" he asked with a jerk of his head toward Gruber.

The German *Fuehrer* began to sputter like a worn-out steam valve. The sputtering rose up to a shrill sound that made Combat think of a noonday factory whistle. Then the *Fuehrer* tried to jerk out his Luger without unsnapping the holster flap. It was perhaps the man's haywire rage that saved Combat's life for a moment. It gave Thirty-Six time to speak.

"I beg of you, my *Fuehrer!*" he cried in a pleading voice. "It will be so much better the other way, *ja?*"

Gruber fumed and fussed and finally simmered down, but the cobra hate in his eyes fairly spat at Combat.

"*Schweinehund!*" he snarled. "You will have plenty of opportunity to think of this moment, later. You would try to find out our secrets, eh? Well, I find it quite pleasing to indulge your curiosity. You shall see a sample of what I have in store for all those who defy my will!"

"A preview of *der Tag?*" Combat hazard as a shot in the dark. "Just what you intend to do with that lousy Formula Q, eh?"

Consternation stamped Gruber's face. He started to speak, but didn't. Combat pressed the advantage. If by a miracle he could bluff them, it might possibly result in their delaying his finish. And every extra minute of life given him was another minute in which to hope for, or possibly make, a break.

"But if it's Formula Q," he said with a shrug, "I wouldn't be interested. We know all about that, you see."

Gruber looked both worried and angry, but once again Thirty-Six stepped forward to soothe him.

"The dog lies, *Fuehrer*," he said quietly. "You have my word on that. Only he and Sir John Drake know anything, and what they do know matters not at all. But Sir John Drake is dead, and Captain Combat will soon join him."

"The same way you killed Sir John?" Combat asked quickly.

Thirty-Six met his eyes and gave him a superior smile.

"My task is not to kill individuals, but nations—empires!" he said harshly.

COMBAT'S HEART sank a bit, and not because of fear for himself. For a moment he thought he had a clue as to Thirty-Six's real identity. If he had been present at Sir John's death, then Thirty-Six was unquestionably one of the dead Bureau chief's staff. Only his staff members could approach him when he was in his office. No, that office clerk must have done it alone. Nor was Thirty-Six one of the two Combat had encountered at his apartment. That is, not unless the mysterious spy possessed the secret powers of reincarnation, because those two at the apartment were as dead as dead men would ever be.

However, the spy's words to Gruber had given Combat another opening. Another chance to sew the seeds of doubt and worry, and he hastened to make the most of it.

"You're slipping, Thirty-Six," he grinned at the spy. "Use your head! I'd be a sap, wouldn't I, to keep the knowledge to myself now that Sir John is dead? I might possibly get killed, too."

"It isn't a possibility, it's a fact," Thirty-Six said calmly. "But I suggest you save your breath. Your prowess in the American art of bluffing is well known to me."

With a smirk for Combat, the spy turned to Gruber and Peiplow.

"There is nothing for us to fear," he said. "May I suggest that we proceed with preparations for the—er—little demonstration. We will not be long in reaching the scene of action, you know."

"Yes, yes, I agree," Gruber said, and bobbed his egg-shaped head up and down. "Whether he bluffs or not I want to make sure that he will not trouble us any more."

Ignoring Combat, the German *Fuehrer* strode aft along the deck. The others followed in his wake, with Combat under the watchful guard of two sailors and a junior officer bringing up the rear. As he was led aft toward the "seal tail" stern deck of the cruiser now under full way, Combat took attentive notice of the boat's construction. And it did not take him long to realize that it was a German craft constructed along the same lines as the British Duchess type of ship.

As the party neared the stern, all interest in the cruiser itself fled Combat like a flash of light. Much activity was taking place, and at first glance Combat had the crazy impression that he was looking at a combination open air torpedo and radio factory. Pointing aft and projecting a few feet out over the stern, was a torpedo launching tube. In the cradle was a torpedo, but a type of torpedo such as Combat had never seen in his life before. It looked more like a miniature submarine with no conning tower.

The driving propeller was at the nose of the thing instead of at the stern, and there were control gadgets fitted along the two sides of the torpedo. And at the extreme end was a round opening, perhaps six or seven inches across. Combat could not see inside the opening, but the bottom lip was silky smooth and tilted down!

To one side of the weird looking torpedo was a huge radio control panel mounted on a revolving platform. Before it, with phones to his ears, was a radio man seated in a sling chair. His feet rested on control pedals so that by pressing one or the other he could swivel himself and the radio panel around to the left or right. And to the radio man's right stood another sailor at the lever controls, by which the strange looking torpedo was launched over the stern of the cruiser.

When the party reached the spot, a deck officer roared out a command and all work ceased instantly while every man almost threw his arm out of joint giving Gruber the Nazi salute. The German *Fuehrer* flipped one back in return, then spread his legs and hooked his two thumbs in his belt and leered at Combat.

"So you know all about our little secret, eh?" he sneered. "Well, suppose you explain it to me? What is that you see there? Tell me just how it works."

COMBAT DIDN'T answer for the moment. He was still too fascinated by the weird-looking object. From where he stood now, he could see that there was a row of small hinge hatches along the starboard side of the missile. Into these two sailors had been placing some of the small boxes of Formula Q taken off the 'Gallant.' As they had put each one inside, they had clamped a chain about it with a link at the end that could be fitted to the chain of the next box. Just how they were placed inside Combat didn't know, for he was standing too far away to see. Somehow, though, the belief came to him that the chain of boxes passed out through the rear opening in the torpedo to form a sort of midget-size mine-boom in the water. "So, it is a little surprise, eh?" Gruber's voice cut in on Combat's thoughts.

The Yank turned to him and nodded. "Pretty little thing. What does it do?"

"Do?" the German leader echoed with a wild laugh. "You shall see a sample of what it will do. *Ja*, there before your swine eyes is what will bring England to her knees and make me complete master of all Europe!"

"Nice work, if you can get it!" Combat cracked.

The German ignored the remark, turned and peered off the port rail. Impulsively the Yank followed his gaze and saw the thin outline of another cruiser far down on the horizon line.

"That is the one, *Fuehrer,*" Thirty-Six's voice spoke up. "Right now our radioman is exchanging signals with her. We will cruise up and down near her and she will never know."

The German leader suddenly grabbed hold of Combat with one hand and pointed with the other at the distant cruiser they were approaching.

"See that?" he shrilled. "There is a *British* cruiser. You shall see her destroyed. *Ja*, you will have a very good view of what goes on. You will see her destroyed, just as all the others will be destroyed on *Der Tag*. And without her navy England is finished. She will not be more than a puppet state of mine!"

As Gruber flung the last at Combat, he whirled around on Thirty-Six.

"There is no need to wait longer!" he barked. "If all is ready, then take charge. You know what to do, and make it very final, you understand?"

"I understand, *Fuehrer,*" Thirty-Six said humbly. Then, taking Combat by the arm, "Come along, Captain," he smiled. "As the *Leader* has promised, you are to have a front row seat. I'm sure you'll be interested for awhile."

A sailor gripping Combat's other arm killed all chances of breaking away. The Yank swallowed the lump in his throat and grinned at the spy.

"Thanks," he said. "But speaking of being interested, just how did you know I had gone aboard the 'Gallant'? Or am I asking too much?"

AS THE spy chuckled before replying, Combat stared hard at him and racked his brain for that elusive bit of memory that would reveal Thirty-Six's identity to him. But although he came close to putting a mental finger on it a dozen times, it continued to escape him.

"How did I know?" Thirty-Six finally answered with a grin. "I really didn't know, for sure. Certainty is quite difficult to establish in my branch of the service. But when I learned that you had killed Lieutenant Jackson, and that you were at Fifty-Nine, I simply put two and two together."

"Meaning?" Combat frowned as they approached the strange looking torpedo.

"Meaning that I never trust one of my agents," Thirty-Six said. "He might be careless, no matter how hard he tried not to be. In short, I assumed that you had learned something from

Jackson. There was a telegram I had sent him. You found it, didn't you?"

"I did," Combat admitted, and experienced a faint trace of admiration for the killer's technique.

"There is the answer to your question," Thirty-Six laughed. "As a simple precaution I *assumed* you had learned something from him. And so I radioed the 'Gallant' in code that should anybody board them that night it would not be Jackson, who was dead, but obviously you. But let me congratulate you, too, Captain. I would have bet much that you would die in your apartment by opening that closet door. Just what happened, though? Naturally I don't know the details. Those two fools died. How did they slip up?"

"Not their fault," Combat grinned, though it was an effort. "They were working for you, so naturally they slipped up. If you get what I mean?"

"Spoken in very bad taste, Captain, considering *your* situation," Thirty-Six chuckled. "You know the American expression about the last laugh, and so forth? I'm going to enjoy that last laugh."

"If you get it!" Combat said grimly.

And as he spoke those words his thoughts flew to Major Stark. Thank God he had told Stark all that he knew. If he died there would still be Fifty-Nine's C.O. to carry on. Yet, what was there for Stark to do? What *could* he do? If only he knew about the Murdock farm! But of course he didn't, and tomorrow, the ninth, was to be *Der Tag?* That information had come from the lips of *Herr* Gruber himself. *Der Tag* for the British Navy and consequently all England.

How did Gruber expect to smash the British Navy?

The question rang through his brain as the sailor halted him and began to remove the cords from his bound arms. With this Formula Q contraption, undoubtedly. But how? How could the Nazis get the entire British fleet? Lookouts would spot those weird torpedoes and most of the ships would be able to veer clear in time. Then too, Germany didn't have enough war craft in the North Sea to do the torpedoing job, and that included U-boats. Then lastly, there were England's own mine fields the Nazis would have to penetrate before getting within striking distance in British waters.

"Your boy friend didn't give me many of the details," Combat said on impulse to Thirty-Six. "Just how does this thing work? Damnedest looking torpedo I've ever seen. Radio controlled, huh?"

"Of course," the super spy nodded. "But it really isn't a torpedo, except in your case. You see, we're willing to waste this one just so... Well, to use another expression, just so you can go along for the ride. Take charge of him!"

Thirty-Six barked the order and then stepped back before Combat could open his mouth. Husky sailors grabbed hold of him, and in the flash of an eyewink he was hoisted up and slapped down on his back, spread eagle style, across the top of the torpedo. He tried to struggle but it was useless. His outstretched arms and legs were lashed about the weird looking missile.

Then he ceased struggling as Thirty-Six came into his view

again. The spy carried a lightweight diving helmet and oxygen tank in his hands, and the smile on his face was like the smile one would see on the face of Satan himself, seated on the throne of hell.

"Yes, a real front row seat, Captain," Thirty-Six said. "There is enough oxygen here to last you until long after we send you over to visit that cruiser. And as you see, the glass face plate will permit you to see everything clearly. The one or two inches of water passing over your head won't blur your vision to any great degree. Perhaps you may be able to raise your head above the water for a better view. Anyway, I'm sure you'll see enough. Goodbye, Captain Combat. It has been an amusing game we've played with each other, though not very exciting... nor very profitable for you, Captain, of course!"

With one last smirk, Thirty-Six slipped the diving helmet over Combat's head and fastened the air-and-water-tight neck-piece securely, while one of the sailors hooked the oxygen tank to the side of the torpedo. The Yank's heart was a lump of lead in his chest as he lay helpless, staring up through the glass plate at the cloudy sky. So this was the end? What a hell of a way to go out! If only he'd really accomplished something for the sake of Sir John's memory. And dammit, if only he could place Thirty-Six's face! He knew damn well he'd seen the man before, and often.

Throbbing sound cut off his thoughts, and the torpedo to which he was lashed started to tremble slightly.

CHAPTER 12
EAGLE ACTION

T HE TREMBLING increased in intensity although the roaring seemed to subside. Teeth clenched and body automatically braced, Bill Combat waited to go hurtling out into the icy waters of the North Sea. Out one side of the face plate of the diving helmet he could see a deck officer with his hand upraised.

Suddenly, Combat saw stark fear spread across that deck officer's face. Then the man cringed and ducked down out of sight. In that same moment shrill screams of terror sliced through the diving helmet to reach Combat's ears. And then, above all the other sound, he heard the sharp yammer of aerial machine gun fire!

Even though the movement might cost him his life, he twisted his helmeted head around to the right and peered desperately through the heavy face glass. The sight that met his straining eyes was like a dream mirage for a fleeting second or so. He just couldn't believe what he saw was true. Yet, it was! A British pursuit plane, a Supermarine Spitfire, was streaking down toward the stern deck of the *Hesse* and spewing out death from all eight of its guns streamlined into the leading edge of the monoplane wing. And on the fuselage of that plane were the markings of Fifty-Nine Squadron.

Perhaps the sailor who did the job of lashing his hands and feet fumbled on the job and made them not half tight enough. Or perhaps sight of that Supermarine Spitfire slicing down filled

Bill Combat with a certain super-strength that comes to each warrior once in a lifetime. At any rate, he jerked and twisted his body around on that torpedo in a wild frenzy of effort, and he was rewarded almost instantly. His right hand came free, and by throwing it across his chest he was able to tear loose the bonds that pinned his left hand.

Though bullets smacked into the deck close by, and the whole world seemed full of screaming sound, he didn't waste a split second turning his head for a look-see. Instead, he lunged up to a sitting position and then forward to where he could reach the ropes about his ankles. His fingernails snapped off and blood spurted from his fingertips, but he ripped and tore at those ropes like a man gone stark, raving insane. And then with a rush they came loose, and he was free.

At that moment he caught the movement of the deck officer leaping toward him out of the corner of his eye. He twisted sharply and kicked up one foot. The German ran his face right straight into that foot and fell sprawling. Combat in the same split second let his own body go limp and half slid and half fell off the opposite side of the torpedo cradle and down onto the deck. No sooner had he hit the deck than he was up on his feet and racing for the rail. He tripped over the radio man, who was dead with Vickers bullets in his brain, and stumbled to his knees. He had tripped because he hadn't seen the crumpled figure. The damn diving helmet still on his head shut off his view.

Cursing, he took precious seconds to rip open the rubber neckpiece and haul the metal and glass globe from his head. No sooner was his head in the open again, than a terrific bedlam of sound crashed against his ear drums. Screams, shouts and wild yells smashed the air all about him, and cutting through it like the voice of doom, itself, the staccato yammer of the strafing plane. Any moment and the shower of death-dealing bullets might slash into that Formula Q torpedo and set off the powerful stuff inside. Sir John had said that friction only would set off Formula Q, but God knew that speeding bullets would set up plenty of friction when necessary.

Any second, any split second, and all hell might blow up there on the waters of the North Sea. Desperately Combat forced his legs into action. Somebody came charging at him from the left. He didn't see the figure clearly, didn't even know whether or not the man had a gun in his hand. He simply half spun and hurled the diving helmet. A bellow of pain told him he had scored a hit. Then he was at the rail and clearing it in a long, running dive.

PERHAPS HE was diving straight down to his death. Perhaps the instant he hit the water the suction of the screws driving that pile of steel armor plates through the waves would drag him in and mangle him to pulp. Perhaps too he might die a long lingering death. The kind that comes after swimming and keeping afloat for hours; until the last tiny drop of strength and the will to keep on struggling has run out of one's body. Yes, perhaps a hundred different kinds of fate awaited him in the waters of the North Sea. They all flashed through his brain as his body curved outward and downward. But if there was any satisfaction to be gained, it was the knowledge that no Nazi hand would pull the rip cord ring on his life in this world.

The break had come, come at the very last minute. He had

not created it. A diving Fifty-Ninth ship had created the break. He had but taken full advantage of it. It was up to him to keep on doing so. Somehow he had to get through this jam. Get out of this tight corner into which death had forced him, and fight with even greater strength to break through the veil of mystery surrounding Formula Q and blast all Nazi hope for *Der Tag* to hell and gone. And he only had from now until dawn tomorrow.

With that truth passing through his brain in letters of fire, his body went slicing down into the water. It seemed years before he could check his plunge, deeper and deeper into the depths of that icy sea. The breath clamped in his lungs seemed to swell up and come close to bursting through the lung walls in an attempt to get free. His head swam and the sea gods pounded his brain with their little white hot hammers. An unseen force tugged gently but surely at his body, and he knew it was the back-lash caused by the cruiser's whirling screws sucking him up toward them.

A year, an eon, an eternity of time dragged by as he fought the suction power of that back-lash and still tried to stay under water. Eventually, though, he could stand the pain in his chest no longer. He had to water-claw for the surface. If the gods brought him up to break surface still within that back-lash area, then there was nothing that he could do about it. God knew it would take just about all of his strength to keep afloat in a calm piece of water.

He broke surface so suddenly that his blurred eyes were unable to grasp that fact until he started to sink under again. Holding back that air in his lungs for one last split second, he got his head above water again and floated flat on his back, spewing out the dead air in his lungs and dragging in great gulps of clean reviving air. The white fires died out in his brain, the throbbing went away, and his arms and legs became parts of him that moved at the command of his brain, and not just lead weights hung on his torso.

He lifted his head and looked around. A sob of relief rose in his throat. The Cruiser *Hesse* was a good half mile away from him, its knife prow peeling off great sheets of white foam from the surface of the water. The strafing plane had ceased diving on the craft. As a matter of fact, an anti-air craft gun aboard the cruiser was dotting the sky all around the Spitfire with balls of flashing red light that changed to great black gobs of smoke which drifted off to be whipped into nothing by the cross winds. AS COMBAT stared at the cruiser he saw something go shooting off the bow. It was a plane, a small cabin seaplane, and it made a beeline toward the east while two more anti-aircraft guns joined the single one and hung a curtain of bursting hell between the seaplane and the Supermarine Spitfire. The British ship, however, made no attempt to break through the curtain of archie bursts. Combat believed that its pilot had not even seen the seaplane leave the cruiser.

"Go get it!" he screamed, one water dripping hand cupped to his mouth. "Gruber's aboard that plane, sure as hell. My God, go after it. Think what getting that stinko will mean! Oh, for the love of God, *go get it*, fellow!"

The British pilot, however, turned away from the barrage thrown up by the *Hesse's* archie guns, and came streaking straight down toward the spot where Combat was bobbing around like a cork. With a hell-roar of sound the diving plane leveled off no more than a dozen feet from the crest of the waves. The pilot shoved open his cockpit cowling and thrust his head and shoulders over the rim of the cockpit as the ship tore by.

A hand waved wildly, and then Combat was able to see the face of the pilot. It was Major Stark, and Fifty-Nine's C.O. was grinning from ear to ear. With an effort Combat waved back and the action made him almost slip down under again. He watched the Spitfire roar past and then zoom slightly. It flattened out at a thousand feet, and then circled about for perhaps two minutes or so. Then it swung around and down.

As the roar of the engine died off into silence Combat blinked and rubbed the water from his eyes with one hand. And when he saw the prop come to a standstill in a horizontal position right straight across the nose of the ship, he let out a wild bellow of alarm.

"That's a land ship, you damn fool!" he shouted, and tried to signal frantically with one hand. "Have you gone nuts? You can't take a Spitfire off water. Stay up there! Radio to some ship to come pick me up!"

No matter how loud he shouted, or how much he waved his arm, neither did him any good. The trim sleek British pursuit job glided down toward the water. When but a few feet above it Stark flattened out of his glide, pulled the nose up to a gentle stall, and then mushed the ship in belly first, with no more splash than you'd cause if you tossed a two-bit piece on a freshly made custard pie. And what was even more perfect, when the plane stopped slushing forward through the water, it was no more than twenty yards from Combat's bobbing head.

Major Stark pulled off his helmet and goggles and stood up on the seat.

"Can I give you a lift, my friend?" he called out cheerily.

COMBAT DIDN'T answer. He saved his strength for the swim, short as it was. At that, Stark had to practically lift him up onto the fuselage and fix him so that his legs dangled down into the cockpit. It took the Yank a minute or two to get his breath. Then he glared at Stark.

"What the hell?" he barked. "Were you dropped when you were a baby? We're both down here, now. Why didn't you radio a nearby ship to come pick me up, huh?"

"I did," Stark grinned. "Got a destroyer not far away. She should be here presently. And me coming down? Well, I had a hunch you'd been through the mill a bit, my lad, and might not have much strength left. No offense, you know, but I had to lift you aboard, you were that pooped, you know. Besides, what the hell's one Spitfire? England has hundreds of them, thousands… I hope. But tell me what…?"

"Hold it!" Combat protested and put up his hands. "You're right, I'm pooped. And thanks for landing. Now, while get my wind back, you tell me your story. How the hell did you find me? And how the hell did you know it was me?"

Stark chuckled and fished a package of cigarettes from his pocket. But after casting his eyes at a couple of floating gobs of oil and raw gas on the water he sighed heavily and stuck the pack back in his pocket.

111

"I didn't, is the answer to both questions," he said. "It was the blooming engine."

"Oh!" Combat growled. "Well, that makes *everything* clear! I should have guessed that, myself. Now, what in hell are you talking about?"

"Easy does it, old boy," Stark grinned. "I'm a terrible story teller, you know. Always begin at the wrong end. Here goes, anyway. Well, I waited up all last night for word from you. None came, but the dawn did, and a lot of blasted fog. Also the trawler fleet had gone out. Well, I was tempted to see the Port Captain and have him radio the fleet for information about you. But on second thought, I didn't. There was a chance it might have spoiled something for you."

"It wouldn't have," Combat grunted. "I'd had the hell kicked out of me long before dawn. But, go on. I want to hear the rest of this."

"So I took some of the lads up on patrol," Stark continued. "I hoped that the fog would clear enough for me to find the fleet. Just what I would have done had I found it, I'm not even sure, now. But a chap does a hell of a lot of things on the spur of the moment when he's worried like the devil, you know."

"Thanks," Combat smiled and leaned forward and pressed the Englishman's arm. "Then what?"

"Well, we stayed out as long as we could, and returned," the C.O. of Fifty-Nine said. "I had my ship re-gassed in a hurry and hopped off again. By the time I was well off shore the fog began to thin in spots, so I started a series of circles, making them bigger and bigger. I saw nothing. I even came miles out into clear air and away from the fog, and still didn't see anything but a cruiser plowing up and down. And then all of a sudden my engine found you for me. I mean, sort of settled things, you know?"

"Listen, pal!" Combat grated. "Just one more unexplained crack about your engine, and…!"

"But it did, really!" Stark protested. "The bloody thing started kicking up something awful. I was dead sure I was due for a nice wet landing down here. Not a pleasant thing, you know, unless, of course… Anyway, the only thing I could do was nose her down toward the cruiser I'd sighted. I thought her English, of course, being in these waters. So I planned to land as near her as I could and let the navy lads fish me out. Damn, what a bloody shame we can't chance a cigarette!"

"I'll buy you a carton when we get on dry land," Combat promised. "So what comes next?"

"A VERY startling discovery," Stark grinned. "In fact, two of them. Two startling discoveries. One that the engine settled back into as sweet a song as you could expect from any engine. Some Nazi propaganda in the carburetor no doubt, and the old girl had to spit it out. Anyway, she started ticking over sweetly again. And then suddenly I noticed some most peculiar business going on on the aft deck of the cruiser. I saw what looked like British sailors, but also some dressed as Germans. And I also saw some lad dressed in the uniform of the R.A.F., but with a damn funny looking hat on his head, tied spread eagle over a damn queer looking torpedo. So I came down for a closer look,

113

and right then a couple of Fritz sailors jumped for a machine gun and started using it."

Stark paused and shrugged.

"Besides not liking that sort of thing," he said, "I became quite sure that chap on the torpedo, or whatever the devil it was, didn't want to stay there. And so, I started strafing the blighters, making sure to keep my burst away from that chap who was hog-tied. You know the rest, and of course you were the chap. Rather a lucky day for us both, eh?"

"For me, plenty!" Combat nodded grimly. "I almost hate to tell you what you missed. That plane that was catapulted off contained none other than little Gruber."

"Gruber?" Stark gasped, his eyes widening.

"In the stinking flesh," Combat affirmed. "If you'd passed me up, you could have got him easy in a Spitfire. And I suspect Hermann Peiplow, and the mysterious Mr. Thirty-Six were with him."

"It could have been the whole blasted Nazi party," Stark said quietly. "You turning into fish food wouldn't have been worth it. Damn, there I go sentimental again. Must do something about it, really. Start crying like a baby in a minute, by God."

"Cry away, pal!" Combat grinned. "To tell the truth, you really should bust me in the nose a few times. I've had some very dizzy thoughts about you since last we met, Stark, old sock."

"Thoughts?" the other echoed. "What thoughts?"

"It was my Intelligence genius trying to jump second gear right into high," Combat laughed. "I almost had you tabbed for Thirty-Six a couple of times."

"What's *that?*" Stark exploded. "Me, Thirty-Six? Why the devil didn't you tell me that while I was still in the air, eh? I'd have landed on you, by God. Seriously, though, what has been happening? Unless I'm mistaken, you've made no mention of it thus far. And you might say I'm the curious type. Damn curious. Good news, eh?"

Combat started to speak but checked himself. Neither of them had seen the destroyer plowing the waves toward them. Combat saw it now, and shook his head at Stark.

"Later," he said and started waving both hands above his head. "And if *this* is something *else* German disguised as British, so help me, I'll resign my commission and take up cutting out paper dolls!"

CHAPTER 13
TANGLED WINGS

D RESSED IN dry uniforms, and with plenty of cigarettes and hard liquor within easy reach, Bill Combat and Major Stark pored over a detail relief map of the northern section of Scotland spread out before them on the office desk of the Commander of the Kinnaird's Head naval base. The last rays of a dying sun slanting through the west windows brought out the deep lines in the Yank's face so strongly they looked as though marked there with a grease make-up pencil. He looked old, and worn out, and deathly tired. That is, save for his eyes. They were like orbs of icy granite with pinpoints of fire glinting in their depths.

He took his eyes from the map a moment and lighted a cigarette. Stark glanced up at him with concern.

"There's a limit to even your strength, old thing, you know?"
he said quietly.

"Yeah, sure," Combat grunted and returned his gaze to the
map. "If it'll make you feel better, I'll go to bed for a month when
this thing is over."

The Yank picked up a pin and stuck it in the map. The hole
made by the pin was surrounded by topographical markings that
indicated hills, ravines, a couple of rivers, and just about enough
level ground to fit in your eye.

"That's Murdock's farm," he said. "At least it was, many, many

years ago. And, incidentally, thank God the Commander here knew his Scottish history, and his northern Scotland. His telling us has saved a lot of time."

Combat paused and glanced out the window at the dying sun.

"And God knows we need all the extra time we can get!" he added. "Well, Stark, what are your ideas?"

"The same as when we started this council of war," Fifty-Nine's C.O. said. "Frankly, get a couple of squadrons of bombers and go up there and blow Murdock's farm right off the bloody map!"

"A swell idea in theory, but not in fact," Combat said, shaking his head. "First, we don't know for sure what's there. We are only guessing. Second, the lads we want might skip away before the first bomb sailed down. Third, if Frankle *is* there we might kill him, and we don't want to do that. I mean, if we blew him to

bits we would never know for sure if by chance the Nazis had sneaked him away to safety. And next, we might kill a lot of innocent Scots. And *that* would look fine in the newspapers, I don't think! Lastly, and perhaps most important of all, blasting the Murdock farm to hell and gone wouldn't necessarily mean that we would knock the props out from Gruber's *Der Tag* plan. Don't you see, Stark, we've got to find out what the *plan* is?"

"Don't we already know?" the C.O. grunted. "From your very recent experiences it's evident the Nazis plan to get British ships with those Formula Q-filled torpedoes."

"That's out, I'm sure of it!" Combat said with a savage shake of his head. "Look, Thirty-Six told me it wasn't exactly a torpedo; that it was only going to be used as one in my case. And look at it from this angle. If it's simply a matter of torpedoing British war craft, an ordinary torpedo will send one of those babies to the bottom. No, this Formula Q thing is something different, something that is many, many times more effective than the regular torpedo."

Combat paused and scowled down at the map without actually seeing it. Stark took that moment of silence to speak again.

"I wonder is what we seek is really up north?" he said. "Don't forget those series of explosions around London and to the south that I told you about."

"I'm not," the Yank said. "I'm making a guess as to what's behind them. It's the old Army game. You attract attention at one place while you're winding up the works for action in some other spot. And here's a point. The Commander here told us that only a skeleton force of the North Sea fleet was on patrol, while the main force is based at Scapa Flow and the Shetlands. They've been there waiting to escort the troop transports to Finland… that never went there."

"And since the *Royal Oak* affair," Stark said sharply, "a fly couldn't get into either base! I know that for a fact, because of my job up here. No, Combat, the Nazis have first got to draw those ships out of the bases before they can do anything with their new torpedo secret."

"That's it, *that's it!*" Combat cried, and thumped Stark on the chest. "That's just what they expect to do at dawn tomorrow! Draw the entire North Sea fleet out into open water!"

"That's what they think they can do, but they can't!" Stark said. "Just how will they destroy the Fleet once it's at sea? No, I can't agree with either of those angles, old man. It's too preposterous and impossible! Look here, why not return to Wick with me and have a go at that trawler, the 'Gallant'? I can have the whole blasted fleet held in port for investigation. We know the 'Gallant' isn't British. That's something to work on. And meanwhile, my chaps can go on patrol and keep an eye on Murdock's farm from the air. Also, we can arrange for armed parties to close in on the place and arrest everybody. Now, *there* is a sensible plan for operation, old man!"

Combat didn't answer immediately. He was battling with his own fears and doubts. True, there was logic in Stark's suggestion, but the plan left too many loopholes through which the enemy could escape. And the most damning thing about it was that it did not guarantee a solution of the mystery. It was simply a means of stopping the mystery from being brought to a head.

In short, it might only result in the Nazis postponing *Der Tag* until a later date… when England had been lulled back to sleep.

He looked at Stark and smiled ruefully. "Guess I come from pretty stubborn stock," he said. "Now wait! Your plan is good, but I can't see that it will get us what we want. I mean that we can be pretty sure the Wick area is lousy with Nazi agents… and no offense to your work, old man. However, if we should return there and start cracking down it would certainly tip them off that we're on to their game. And the hell of it is, we *aren't*. But if they thought we were, they would pull out like rats leaving a sinking ship, and our only prize would be the 'Gallant' and its crew, from whom we might or might not learn something. The big secret would still be a secret we hadn't solved. And the entire affair would just be postponed. See what I mean?"

"Unfortunately, I do," Stark growled.

"Now, your returning alone is perfectly okay," Combat pressed his point. "You can say you force-landed in the water and the destroyer picked you up, just as it did. Leave my name out of it. You still haven't the faintest idea what happened to me after I went down to row out to the 'Gallant'."

"And the idea of that?" Stark quizzed as the Yank paused.

"Thirty-Six and his band of cutthroats!" Combat said grimly. "Unless I'm mistaken as hell, Thirty-Six is going to move heaven and high water to find out if I survived that little North Sea experience. They didn't tell me much aboard the *Hesse*, but Gruber did shoot off his yap a bit. Also, I've got a couple of eyes in my head. Anyway, I think that Thirty-Six is just a wee bit worried about me, right now, and if he's got agents around

Wick and Fifty-Nine, he's going to have the boys check up on me. That's your job. Tell the crazy story of what you saw. Let it be known that it doesn't make sense to you. Say that an archie sliver got your gas feed line, and that you were able to SOS for help before you landed. It's a cinch the *Hesse's* operator did pick up your SOS. And that will make Thirty-Six feel much, much better."

"Of course, you're right," Stark nodded. "But I still don't see why...."

"Here's why," Combat cut in. "There's one thing Thirty-Six doesn't know, or I'll eat my shirt—that the 'Gallant's' captain let slip about Murdock's farm and that I was to go there and report orders from Berlin to some bird known as Agent Four. Even if Thirty-Six contacts the 'Gallant's' captain, you can be sure the louse won't say a word, even if he should remember. He has no desire to taste Thirty-Six's anger and the punishment to follow. If it's the last thing he does, it'll be to cover up any slip of his tongue."

"So that would leave the chaps at Murdock's farm unsuspecting?" Stark murmured.

"Right," Combat nodded. "And perhaps still expecting those orders from Berlin. That's my in. I'm still taking orders to Agent Four, whoever the hell he is."

"Bloody risky, I'd say!" Stark scowled. "You're just going to fly in there... not even knowing where the landing field is, and in the dark, too... and just say, 'Look, chaps, which one of you is Agent Four?' Is that what you plan?"

Combat grinned and poured a couple of drinks. The liquor

took most of the scowl from Stark's face. Presently the C.O. smiled a bit sheepishly.

"Then how the devil *do* you plan to do it?" he wanted to know.

Combat made him wait until he'd finished his own drink. Then he leaned forward and spoke in a low voice for a few minutes. When he'd finished, Stark helped himself to another drink and expelled air through his lips in a soft whistle of incredulity.

"To borrow one of your Yank expressions," he said, "you're a bit of a fool for getting bashed about, what?"

Bill Combat touched a lump on his head that instantly started throbbing with pain.

"They can't kick any more hell out of me than they already have," he said grimly. "And this time I'll take measures to protect myself. After all, it will be my own doing this time."

"Or *undoing!*" Stark said with emphasis.

"I'll have to take that chance," Combat grinned. "But listen, Stark, old sock, I don't want you to think I'm trying to grab all the play. We're teammates in this thing, and if you earnestly disagree...."

"It wouldn't matter a bloody damn," Stark said and laughed. "I think I know you, old chap. You'd go off on your own, anyway. No, I won't disagree, really. I'll just wish you all the luck in the world, and for God's sake, be careful. But I do wish like the devil there was something *I* could do!"

"There is," Combat; said in a sober tone. "You'll return to the squadron as soon as you can, and spread the story we've agreed on. However, you'll keep your eyes open, and watch the trawler fleet in particular. I don't think there are any others like the 'Gallant,' but I don't believe I'd want to bet on it. And if by chance...."

Combat let his voice trail off.

"And if by chance, what?" Stark prompted.

"If by chance I don't show up by dawn," the Yank said slowly, "then you carry out your idea. Have that trawler fleet nailed in port. Send up your lads to scout the Murdock farm. And... send in land parties to see what the hell happened to me. But nothing is going to happen to me, dammit—it can't!"

Stark stared out the window and across Scotland to the red sunset.

"If the prayers of all England mean anything, nothing will," he murmured softly.

CHAPTER 14
DARK DANGER

B LACK NIGHT had come to northern Scotland. There were a few clouds, but not enough to blot out the winking stars completely. Yet their combined light failed to touch the panorama of night-shadowed ground that rolled by under Bill Combat's plane. He flew a Spitfire that the Kinnaird base Commander had borrowed for him from a nearby squadron, and as he flew a compass course through the night, he felt a pang of sympathy and sorrow for the sleek, speedy ship. Being a born airman, the Yank had the same love for airplanes that some men have for horses. To him a ship was not just an airplane, a man-made contraption of metal and wood and fabric. It was something almost human, something alive that responded to his every command and bidding. Without it he was landlocked, dependent entirely upon himself. But with it he was on a par with real eagles, and the master of anything under his steel claws, known as Vickers guns.

On impulse he reached out his free hand and patted the cockpit rim.

"It'll be tough, old girl," he grunted. "Makes me feel like a heel, but it's the only way."

Combat checked his instrument panel for the hundredth time. He was right on the beam, as it were, and in another few minutes he should spot the "S" turn in a river that marked the southern boundary of the ancient and almost legendary Murdock farm.

As time for action drew near, his heart picked up its beat and the blood started pounding through his veins. Outwardly, though, he was calm, cool and collected. He had planned and plotted every move he was going to make. He had worked the whole thing out in his own mind. All that was left was to keep to schedule—right on the old button. When the "S" turn in the river was but a mile away, and he could just barely see the faint glow of the stars reflected on its surface, he snapped off his instrument panel light and moved a thumb up to the radio mike button.

He had no way of telling how Nazi agents, disguised in R.A.F. uniform, got into Murdock farm at night, but he had a hunch they undoubtedly signaled their approach and identity by code radio dots and dashes. As a result of that, those on the ground would not put out landing flares by mistake… if they did use landing flares.

However, Combat naturally didn't know the approach code, but it was necessary to start faking a message before taking his next step. And so he started jabbing the radio mike button in a meaningless jumble of dots and dashes. Then he stopped short and shoved the Spitfire down in a wing-howling power dive that must have been heard clear across Scotland. When he had dropped a couple of thousand feet, he deliberately worked the throttle so that the engine sputtered and spit and shot long tongues of flame out the exhausts. Then he choked the engine so that it made an even greater racket, meanwhile flopping the ship from side to side.

But no signs of landing flares met his steady gaze. And he was not really disappointed. He hadn't expected every break, and he felt pretty sure that the "keepers" of Murdock farm would be dead certain a pilot aloft was one of them before they'd reveal their secret landing field. However, Combat stuck to his stunt until he was too low to do anything else but take the next step in his plan.

Making the engine stutter just once more, he cut off the switch and hauled the throttle all the way back. Then, with his head stuck out of the opened cockpit cowling, he guided the ship down toward the mass of uninviting shadows below. When tree tops seemed ready to tangle with his prop, he flipped on his landing lights for a split second. Mercifully, they showed a parting between two clusters of trees, and a short stretch of flat but rock-studded ground beyond.

To indicate that his landing lights had also failed him, he snapped them off and headed blind for the opening in the trees. Long seconds dragged by as the Spitfire slid forward at practically a stalling speed. Then, as Combat felt tree branches slash against both wingtips, he nosed down just a bit for sufficient gliding speed to carry him through the opening. Then, finally, he hauled the ship up to a slow stall. The last thing he did, before the plane mushed down like a dead body, was to bury his head in his arms, twist sidewise in the cockpit.

He had left the wheels up, of course, and so the Spitfire cracked the ground in a glancing blow on its smooth belly. The ship bounced once, then came down hard to earth again. Its right wingtip connected with one of the rocks, that jutted above the ground, then ground-looped the plane like a spinning top. Just how it settled to earth again, Combat didn't know. The fire works went off in his head as his body absorbed the full force of the shock.

WHEN ALL movement ceased, Combat stayed right where he was, half pinned under the wreck. He had planned this crash, and he had known that he was going to take quite a beating. But he hadn't known that his strength and general ability to absorb punishment was at a much lower ebb than he had believed. And so, in those first few minutes after the Spitfire struck, he didn't give a damn if the whole blasted German Army was running all over the British Isles. All he wanted to do was relax and go to sleep and wake up a hundred years from now.

However, the aches and pains and sense of utter weariness subsided considerably as the minutes ticked by, and he came back a bit along the road to normalcy. He snapped out of his trance and made himself as comfortable as he could, without getting out of the wreck. He strained his ears for any sounds about him. At first he thought he heard a million different sounds. But this, he realized, was only his imagination doing tricks. He continued listening.

At the end of ten minutes his ears were ringing like four alarm fire bells. He thought he would go nuts if *something* didn't happen. Had his plan fallen flatter than yesterday's sponge cake? Was this trip to Murdock's farm, and this crash just a waste of time? Had Drake's plan really been the best?

He cursed through clenched teeth to drive away these taunting thoughts. And then, a sound did come to his ears. The sounds of persons running through underbrush, and calling to each other! He let his head droop slightly, but kept his eyes open. A few seconds later, a disc of light moved across the ground, then halted on the wreckage of his plane. A thick voice called out: "Here it is! I have found it!"

More discs of light joined the first and presently Combat saw four pairs of booted feet standing close to him. Then hands reached down and touched him. One hand felt his pulse, another fumbled for his heart.

"He's alive!" a voice said. "We'll lift him out. *Lieber Gott,* it's a wonder he lived through it. Look at how the plane is crashed!"

Other voices agreed, but Combat didn't pay attention. He felt like shouting for joy at the top of his lungs. Two words, *Lieber*

Gott, had banished the heart-gnawing fear that his rescuers were merely honest Scotsmen. Scotsmen don't say *Lieber Gott* when they get excited. The truth was established. There *were* Nazis at Murdock's farm!

A moment later, however, some of his joy was banished. "Who is he, do you suppose?" he heard a voice ask. "If he has no business here, others may come searching for him. And there is not much time until dawn."

"We'll take care of that," a harsher-sounding voice snapped. "We'll hide the wreck under the trees, and if we find he is English when he wakes up… why then there'll be only one thing for us to do. Come on, lift him up. Wait! He is perhaps coming around, now."

As they had picked him up, and turned him over so that his face was to the light, Combat purposely opened his eyes. He forced a dazed and glassy look into them which wasn't particularly difficult to do. And he struggled weakly to release the grip they had upon him.

"Agent Four," he mumbled in slurring German. "Must contact… Agent Four. I… I… orders from… Berlin…."

He let his voice trail off into silence, closed his eyes and let his whole body go limp. It was difficult to keep it limp and lifeless in the burst of voices that smote his ears.

"Mein Gott! The one we expected last night!" cried one of the Germans.

"But Thirty-Six said he was killed. He told us so when he radioed the hour for us to expect our comrades in those English planes!" cried another.

"Perhaps he is another that Thirty-Six has sent at the last minute?" a third ventured.

"We will get nowhere babbling on like this!" grated the harsh voice of the obvious leader. "We will take him up to the place and revive him as quickly as possible. *Gott*, we were fools to have been so careful and not to have shown him the landing place when we failed to understand his signals. Give a hand, all of you. We will take him up to the place. We can take care of the wreck later, or even leave it as it is. It won't matter. But we must find out if he has new orders for us!"

There was no longer an ache, or a tiny bit of pain, or even a single trace of fatigue in Combat, as the group of men carried him gently over the rough ground. All that was gone. Success, at last, had driven it away and filled him full of new strength and new hope, and a new determination to smash through to a complete and final victory. In fact, it was all he could do to keep a thoroughly contented smile off his lips. However, he managed to do that for the simple reason that one of the men kept putting the flashlight beam on his face to see if he had regained consciousness again.

AND SO he kept his eyes shut, his face and body relaxed and tried to picture in his own mind the terrain over which they carried him. As far as he could make out, they had traveled up a brush and tree covered hill right after leaving the spot where he had crashed. At some point up that hill, though, the party turned to the right and continued around the hill and came out on what seemed to be a fair-sized plateau of ground. They walked along this for a spell, then started down a gradual slope to the left. Just before they started down the slope Combat's pulse quickened. He wasn't definitely sure, but he was almost positive that he smelled gas and oil, such as are used in high powered engines.

Airplane engines? Were there planes on this secret landing field that he had completely missed in the dark? That thought flashed through his brain. And then he forgot about it for the time being. The party had come to a halt. He risked a quick opening of his eyes and caught a flash glance of the face of a cliff. There was an opening, with actual doors, but from fifty feet away they would have been completely invisible, because of the trees and vine growth that cut them from view.

"Wait here," the harsh-voiced leader said. "I will go in and speak to the fool. I'll tell him it's a messenger from the King, who crashed while trying to land."

The rest of the group growled in agreement. Combat heard but did not see the heavy doors open. The pest with the flashlight had turned for another look at his face and he had been forced to close his eyes. In less than a moment, however, the harsh-voiced leader had reappeared.

"Bring him in and lay him on the couch," he ordered. "You, Karl, get him some brandy. We may be able to revive him with that. Careful, now. He may be more badly hurt than we think."

For one crazy moment, Combat was possessed with the almost uncontrollable desire to burst out laughing. Flirting with possible instant death though he was, the situation nevertheless had its humorous side. Here Nazi agents were falling all over themselves in an effort to preserve his well being. Did they but realize who they carried so tenderly through the opened doors of that cliff face, they would probably drop dead from stunned amazement.

Combat was carried inside and placed gently on a couch. A glass of brandy was put to his lips and his wrists and neck were massaged. He permitted a little of the brandy trickle down his throat, then started choking and groaning. The cup of brandy was taken away.

He opened his eyes, then, and stared vacantly at the ring of anxious faces before him.

A vacant stare in his eyes, yes, but that was for their benefit. Actually he took in everything within range. He was inside a well furnished room. A huge combination living room and bed room, built into the hill. There were bunks along the walls, plus chairs, tables and an assortment of other pieces of furniture. On the far side, opposite him, was a door leading into another room. It was partly open and he could see things beyond in that room that quickened his pulse. It was fitted up as a chemist's laboratory.

And it was only then that he became conscious of the faint smell of chemicals in his nose.

He swept all that in a single glance, then brought his eyes back to the ring of faces before him. They were not bad looking faces. Very English looking, in fact. Five men in all faced him, and stared at him with anxious eyes. Four wore uniforms representing various branches of England's fighting forces. The fifth was in civilian clothes, shabby clothes that were badly stained and spotted, and in need of pressing.

When Combat looked into the face of that man, that civilian, he came within an ace of giving himself away by stiffening violently.

In the nick of time, though, he checked himself and clamped down hard on his nerves. God help him if he failed himself, now. His search was over. Sir John had been absolutely right. Varden Frankle was alive, for there he stood, with hairless head, shaggy eyebrows, wrinkled face and all!

CHAPTER 15
AGENT FOUR

"SPEAK TO me! You have come from the King? We are beating the Germans, yes? The King said I helped a lot, didn't he? And what about the German spies? They haven't found out where I am hiding, have they?"

The babbling voice of Varden Frankle shattered the silence of the room. His voice was high and shaky, like the voice of a terrified child of ten. Combat looked at the man but continued to keep the blank and dazed look on his own face. Inwardly he was on fire. He wanted to leap to his feet and tear the very hearts out of the other four. He didn't have to know the details; he could fill in the story with guesses that he felt sure came damned close to the truth. Just how the Nazi rats had actually done it, he did not know. But he did know what they *had done!*

Damn their stinking souls, they had posed as English protectors who would keep him safe and sound and hidden where the Nazis could not get him. And probably filled him full of hokum about how he could serve the king of the country which had protected him all these years since the day he had fled his beloved Vienna. And having created that belief in the old man's mind, they had got him to produce his secret Formula Q *for them to use!*

As though fate had selected that moment for Combat to learn the reason why Varden Frankle still lived, the chemist spoke again.

"Is it the same request you bring from the King?" he shrilled and waggled a finger at Combat. "If so, my answer is still *NO*. I love your King, I love your country, but I shall never reveal my formula to anybody. No, not even to those who protect my life. I cannot, I must not. What two men know is not a secret. One of them might not keep it a secret. My secret is too terrible to risk falling into the wrong hands. No, I will produce Formula Q for you, but I will not tell even the King my secret. Nor will I leave England. I have lived here, and I shall die here. If Gruber defeats England and comes here to England, then it will be useless to flee elsewhere. I will be glad to go to my God!"

Combat's heart ached with pity for the poor man. One of the Nazis, the leader, no doubt, moved over to the man and put one arm about his shoulder. Combat could have leaped to his feet and knocked the German dead.

"Calm yourself, Frankle, old fellow," he soothed in a voice typically Londonish. "His Majesty understands how you feel, and he has promised not to make the request again. Of course not! This courier simply came up to bring personal greetings from the King, and to thank you for all your wonderful work. But he has crashed in his airplane, and is a sick man. We must take care of him. Now, why don't you go back to your work. There are still many of the bombs to be packed, and the planes to take them away will be here in a few hours. Jack, here, will help you. You'll go back to work for the King, eh?"

The old man sighed softly and nodded.

"Yes," he said, turning away from the group. "I will go back to my work. As you say, there is much to do. We must not fail the King."

The Nazi leader gave him a friendly pat on the shoulder, then jerked his head meaningly at a short, stocky, sandy-haired man. The sandy-haired one followed Frankle through the door on the opposite side of the room. Instantly the leader turned to Combat. He put a finger to his lips and flashed a warning from his dark eyes.

"Speak only English!" he hissed. "I am Agent Four. What have you to report?"

It was some of the toughest acting Combat had ever done in his life, and his heart was in his throat as he fixed his blank stare on Agent Four's face. He blinked, shook his head slightly, and drew a shaking hand down the side of his face.

"Agent Four," he said in a thick voice. "Who is Agent Four? Where am I? Where is the *Kommandant, the Staffel Kommandant!* Am I not supposed to go out on patrol against the swine Eng…?"

A hand was clapped over his mouth before he could finish the last word. Agent Four swore softly and looked miserable.

"Don't talk!" he said sharply to Combat. "Here, take some more brandy. It will help. You must have received a bad knock on the head. You're still dazed. Here, have some more brandy and rest. You will be all right in a minute or two. You've got to be!"

There was the desperation of a very worried and upset man in those last four words. Grinning inwardly, Combat took some more of the brandy, and then let his body slump back on the couch. Agent Four watched him anxiously and kept locking and unlocking the fingers of his two hands.

"What else does one do for crash shock?" he asked helplessly of the other two. "We know he came to report to me. He said so while he was still half unconscious. And now he doesn't know anything about any Agent Four."

"And he said, 'Orders from Berlin', too!" breathed one of the other Nazis.

"Do you suppose there is a change of plans, a delay?" asked the third in an awed voice.

"How do I know?" the leader said viciously. "But there can't be any change. That is impossible! Everything is ready, and has been for days. In a short time the planes will arrive and collect the stores of Q bombs. Zero Hour is at dawn. No, everything is ready. I'm sure there is no change. But we must find out what he has to report. Give him some more brandy. Get some water. Perhaps bathing his face will help. We've *got* to make him talk!"

COMBAT ALLOWED them to work over him for a good ten minutes before he showed any signs of regaining full control of his senses. And during those minutes a million and one thoughts raced through his brain. He couldn't keep up the sham forever. There were things he had to learn; things he had to find out, somehow. Before starting out on this wild venture there had been the faint idea in his brain that he might be able to learn the truth from Frankle, himself. Or at least get the chance to snoop around and find out things on his own hook… and then knock everything into a cocked hat.

That hope, now, though, had gone higher than a kite. Varden Frankle was alive, but he realized he would learn nothing from this half insane genius—even though he managed to get him off alone. And, as for snooping around on his own? What a chance, what a hope! Not only had his slick idea got him into the inner den of Nazi intrigue, it had practically made him the most important personage there. Not unless he dropped dead would those Nazis watching him let him out of their sight.

There was but one other way to gain what he sought. Bluff. Bluff his fool head off. Play right up to their own game, and pray like hell he'd get places. In other words, get them to *tell him* what it was all about. Tell him, and not realize they were telling him. And so, breathing an inward plea to Lady Luck to stick close, he weakly brushed their hands aside.

"Give me some brandy," he said and rubbed a hand across his forehead. "I feel like I've been having a terrible nightmare. I crashed, didn't I?"

He looked at Agent Four as he spoke the question. The Nazi nodded vigorously and the worry dropped from his face in chunks, almost.

"Yes," Agent Four said. "You started to signal us when something went wrong with your set. Then your engine failed. We didn't dare put out landing flares, as we didn't know. You crashed in the darkness. I am the one you seek."

Combat let suspicion creep into his eyes. He must be sure to play the game right up to the hilt.

"And your…?" he began in German.

Agent Four almost fainted and furiously gestured for silence. "Speak English!" he whispered fiercely. "I told you once, but you were still suffering from the crash shock. The one we keep here must hear only English. Were you not told?"

Combat's heart skipped a beat at the steely tone that had come into the man's voice. Play the game to the hilt, huh? Better watch his step or he'd play the game right into a face full of Luger bullets.

"He is still here, then?" he asked in wide eyed surprise. Then sharply, "Wait! And what is *your* number?"

The Nazi blinked.

"It is Four," he said. "When you were unconscious you called it out. You came to report to me, did you not?"

Combat hesitated, then took a chance to make his position doubly believable in their minds.

"I was assigned to the task of one who was killed last night," he said. "Two hours ago I was aboard the trawler 'Gallant.' Does that mean anything to you?"

Agent Four's face became alive with excitement. He turned around for a second, saw that the door leading into the laboratory was closed and then turned back to Combat.

"Everything!" he hissed. "You bring orders from Berlin, eh?"

"First," Combat said sternly. "What were your last orders?"

"They were from Thirty-Six, himself," Agent Four said. "Early this evening by radio. He ordered me to be ready for the British

137

planes that will arrive tonight. We are to load them with the Q bombs. The 'Gallant' and the other trawler will be waiting at Wick. They will meet the destroyers and U-boats at a certain place off shore."

As the Nazi paused for breath, Combat slowly nodded his head and stroked his chin, as though in deep thought. And he was in deep thought, beyond all doubt! British planes to pick up bombs? Two trawlers waiting at Wick? Nazi U-boats and destroyers waiting at some secret rendezvous off Scotland's shores? The questions hammered through his brain.

A sudden thought came to him and he took a long chance with his next question.

"Did Thirty-Six change the time of Zero Hour?" he asked.

"No," Agent Four said promptly. "It remains the same. Two hours before dawn."

The Nazi suddenly stopped and leaned toward Combat.

"But Berlin has changed the hour?" he whispered. "My suggestion has been accepted and it is an hour sooner?"

"*Your* suggestion?" Combat echoed in a half scornful and half puzzled tone.

"Yes," Agent Four replied. "My suggestion. I suggested that it be made an hour sooner. There are enough of the Q bombs already cached at Wick. And the 'Gallant' has three of the guide torpedoes in her hold. I suggested that the 'Gallant' leave an hour sooner and contact the U-boats and destroyers. They can send out one of the mine-booms while the planes are taking the rest of the Q bombs from here. That will only take an hour."

Combat felt as though his hair was standing up on end.

Mine-booms! So his guess aboard the *Hesse* had been correct! And Thirty-Six had not lied when he'd said that the queer-looking torpedo was not really a torpedo. So it was loaded with a chain mine-boom. It was launched over the side and its course controlled by radio. When the torpedo had reached a certain point, the chain mine-boom could be made to come out the opened rear end of the torpedo.

"My suggestion has been adopted, eh?" Agent Four's eager question broke into Combat's thoughts.

The Yank hesitated a moment, then figuratively crawled way out to the very end of the limb.

"It has been neither adopted nor rejected, according to my orders," he shrugged. "It is obvious, now, that Thirty-Six has been too busy to contact you again by radio. That is why the new order was sent to the Gallant for relaying to you."

"New order?" Agent Four exploded.

"A new order!" Combat said in a harsh voice. "You are to continue with your work, but the time when the Leader shall strike has been postponed twenty-four hours!"

Agent Four rocked back on his heels and the expression that spread over his face was as though Combat had belted him right on the nose. Stunned silence settled over the room, broken only by a faint whirring sound that came through the closed door of Varden Frankle's Formula Q laboratory.

Then suddenly the silence was broken more forcibly by the roar of an airplane engine somewhere up in the night sky above them.

CHAPTER 16
WINGS FROM HELL

A S THE sound of that plane came down to their ears, each man looked at the other, and Combat's puzzled frown was quite genuine, too. Then Agent Four stirred himself. He moved toward the doors in the face of the cliff.

"Wait here," he directed Combat and the two others. "I will see if it is friend or enemy."

The inspiration to get up on his feet and tell Agent Four he'd go along with him, shot through Bill Combat. But before he could put it into action, however, the Nazi had slipped through the doors and was gone. The Yank sat back and took a sip of brandy to cover up any telltale expression that might be showing on his face. His nerves were singing high C, and the familiar clammy sensation was stealing across the back of his neck.

So close, yet so far! Was that to be the case?

With a respite of twenty-four hours, he was positive he could do much there at the Nazi secret hide-out. That was why he had taken the long shot chance and informed Agent Four that *Der Tag* had been delayed one whole day. God, yes! Give him just twenty-four measly hours and he could tie the Nazi plot on Scotland's shore into knots. Simple, too. The trawler fleet could be held in port. British navy ships could go after the U-boats and German destroyers lurking off shore. An intensive search of Wick would result in the cached Formula Q bombs being found. And a single Fifty-Nine ship could ride herd on this Nazi hide-out.

Combat dismissed his thoughts for a moment and listened intently to the sound of the ship out in the night air. Could that be Stark coming to look for him again? He prayed that if it were Stark the man would not try to land.

As though the war gods were answering his prayers, the Yank heard the sound of the plane engine grow fainter and fainter. It was going away. *It was going away!* He felt as though he had to say something or bust. The two Nazi agents left with him were studying him with polite curiosity. He returned their stare and jerked a thumb toward the sky.

"You often hear planes that have no right here?" he asked.

"Never before until two days ago," one of them answered him. "Two days ago there was one plane that circled above us constantly. I can tell you it worried us a lot. At one time he came down to within five hundred feet of us. Had we had a machine gun I would have shot him down. He saw nothing, I guess, because he did not come back yesterday."

"But he did today!" Combat said to himself. Then aloud, "Ten thousand pilots could not spot this place. It is perfectly hidden."

The other Nazi chuckled and made gestures with his two hands.

"And what it contains—what is here!" he said in a hoarse voice. "One little *poof* and this whole hill would be nothing but a great huge crater in the ground. But I shall be glad when I am relieved of duty here, though. That Frankle gives me the creeps. Sometimes I almost think he suspects, and is secretly planning something."

"Rubbish!" snarled the other Nazi. "He simply thinks we are

trying to discover his secret process. But we gave that up long ago. I am ashamed of myself, though. I rank with the finest explosive chemists in the world, yet his process baffles me. And I have watched him closely day after day, too!"

"And I, also," sighed his companion. "When I think of the reward that is ours should we discover the secret, I want to...."

The rest was cut off short. At that exact split-second the cliff doors were thrown open. Two men in British uniform stepped quickly into the room. One was Agent Four. There was berserk rage on his face and a Luger in his hand. The Luger pointed square at the middle of Bill Combat's stomach. The Yank hardly noticed Agent Four or his gun. His gaze was riveted on the second English uniformed officer who entered.

The man was Agent Thirty-Six!

For five full seconds the picture remained as it was. Then Agent Four made a jerking motion with his Luger, and snapped an order to his two men.

"Take his gun!" he commanded.

"Keep clear in case I have to shoot!" Even if Combat had wanted to be wild, reckless and absolutely nuts, he wouldn't have stood a chance of doing anything. In movements faster than light, the two Nazi whirled, pinned him down on the couch and took his service automatic from its holster. Then they stepped back, their own guns in their hands, and glared at him frosty-eyed. The Yank didn't give them a single glance. Since the very beginning his eyes had not once left Agent Thirty-Six's face.

Truth had crashed down on his brain in a stunning blow. That alone was why he had not even attempted a struggle. Truth is truth! The Yank had been stunned into partial paralysis. Number Thirty-Six was no longer a man of mystery to Bill Combat. God, no! And he had met the man many times. And there he stood. The trick mustache that hid his mouth was gone. And so were some of the other make-up touches. There he stood as Combat had really known him.

Colonel Wilson, aide to General Books of R.A.F. Staff!

FOR ONE crazy instant Combat's taut nerves almost let go in small pieces, and hysterical laughter gurgled up in his throat. He wanted to shout and hear his own voice. To pinch himself and feel pain. Anything to make sure he was not dreaming, or stark raving insane. But there was no necessity for him to do either. The English traitor stepped forward a pace or so and smiled down at him sardonically.

"The surprise is mutual, Captain Combat," he said in a perfectly controlled and accented voice. "Greetings, though, nevertheless."

Combat sat up slowly, oblivious to the suddenly hopeful gleam that leaped into the eyes of the Nazis on either side of him. He stared hard and long at Colonel Wilson, and all the contempt and disgust he had ever felt in his whole life was in his stare. Then finally he spoke, each word sounding like steel striking steel.

"This makes everything clear," he said. "No wonder you were always ten jumps ahead of us. No wonder every damned thing leaked out! There was a stinking louse in the woodpile. You!"

Colonel Wilson flushed to roots of his hair, but he soon had his anger under control. He bowed mockingly to Combat.

"Thanks for the compliments, Combat," he said. "Of course, I was always ten jumps ahead of you, as you so quaintly put it. When I assumed my position in the… well, the affairs of the world… I had not the intention of filling it in any slip-shod manner. Your other remark does not interest me, however. The old order of things is dead and done for. I serve no nation, no particular group of people. I serve an ideal, and that ideal shall triumph. In your eyes I am a traitor, eh? A Benedict Arnold to the land of my father, and…?"

"No, not that!" Combat cut in with a voice that struck like a lash. "No, because I don't believe you ever found out who your father was, did you?"

The Yank didn't give a damn what he said. In that moment he would have liked nothing better than for the English traitor to rush him. Just two seconds with his hands about the man's throat and the other Nazis in the room could fire their Lugers until hell froze over. Colonel Wilson's face went red with fury, but he made no move to avenge Combat's insult. He simply stood where he was until his anger was once more under control. Out the corner of his eye, Combat saw sad disappointment on Agent Four's face.

Then Number Thirty-Six spoke again. His voice was light, almost kidding. But there was the tone of death underneath.

"This place," he said with a short wave of his arm, "is almost a luck charm for me. It was here, also, that I caught another one of your fools. Sir John spoke of him to you. I refer to Agent Roberts. He was far more clever than you, though. He was here with us for three days before my suspicions were confirmed."

"Not the way I heard it," Combat taunted as the man paused. "It was von Berne who got the credit for unmasking Roberts. In fact, von Berne admitted it to me that day he died."

The Yank's blind shot hit the English traitor's vanity. The man stiffened and his voice rang with snarling indignation.

"If so, then von Berne lied to you!" he blazed. "Von Berne worked under my orders. It was I who decided to lead Roberts into a trap that would mean the end of him. I knew he planned to seek Sir John's aid that day. So I arranged that flight in the sport plane. I arranged for von Berne to fly out to sea and contact a U-boat. That U-boat would slip in close to Plymouth and test our Q guide torpedo. I selected von Berne and Roberts for the job, and...."

"Roberts didn't recognize you?" Combat blurted out in spite of himself.

The German master spy gave him a pitying look.

"Naturally not, you fool!" he clipped out. "This is the first time that anyone but my Leader has seen me as you see me now. No, Roberts had not the faintest idea. Of that I am sure. However, when I selected him to go with von Berne, he didn't dare do anything but go. Too bad they didn't contact that U-boat. I had quite a nice reception planned for him. He must have become suspicious en route. Von Berne must have let something slip. Anyway, he bungled the job and they both died. Roberts should have sent those Formula Q pellets he stole to Sir John by mail."

Colonel Wilson enjoyed a little laugh at his own joke, and then shrugged.

"Perhaps, though, he planned to use them instead of a gun

on von Berne when the right moment came," he murmured. "That we'll never know. And frankly, I'm not interested. Well, Combat, you escaped me once, but there is not going to be any second time. Nor any elaborate ceremony, either."

"Gruber won't like your enjoying it all by yourself," Combat said to him. "And, after all, he's the top man."

"*Der Fuehrer* will be perfectly satisfied just to learn of your death!" the master spy snapped. "But I am not a man to deny credit where credit is due, Combat. Had I not flown up here for a last minute check, *Der Tag* might not be as successful as we want it to be—and as it shall be. However, for your own information, had I not come and learned the truth from Agent Four, here, when I landed, it would have made little difference. Our plans are too far advanced. England meets her doom within a few hours."

"Sounds big, Wilson," Combat said. "But I don't think England wants to meet her doom, if you get what I mean. True, we don't know all of your cute little plans, but we know enough. Those Q bombs are going to stay right where they are in Wick. And the 'Gallant' and the other trawler are not going to sail. You've forgotten one thing in your plans."

If Combat expected to see a shade of worry pass through Thirty-Six's eyes his hope fell down with a crash. The spy laughed softly.

"Really, Combat?" he mocked. "Suppose you tell me, then I can take care of it."

"Sure," the Yank grinned at him. "Fifty-Nine Squadron. I didn't come into this blind, you see. If you've just come from

Fifty-Nine after another of your routine visits, maybe you noticed that the 'Gallant' was still with the fleet, eh?"

"I did," Wilson nodded. "And her presence there more or less proved to me that you had drowned this afternoon."

"That's what I figured *you'd* figure," Combat shot at him. "I didn't drown, as you can see. Unless I show up at Fifty-Nine before dawn, not a trawler will be permitted to leave its harbor. Land parties will be headed for this spot to bottle you up, and Fifty-Nine's pilots will ride herd on this spot and machine gun any bird who so much as sticks his nose out into the open. Now, what do you think of that, eh? Looks like we're both out on the limb doesn't it? And that *Herr* Gruber's *Der Tag* is going to be quite a flop?"

"It means nothing of the sort," Wilson said quietly. "And I'm very sorry that I cannot join you out on the limb. My compliments again for thoroughness of preparation, but I took all that into consideration too!" He paused a moment and fixed Combat with his eyes.

"You fool!" he shouted. "Do you think I play this game like a child? No. I am the one who has been thorough. I have made sure that nothing will stand in the way of *Der Fuehrer's* success tomorrow. Would you like to know how?"

Combat started to speak, but he didn't for a second. At that moment he had seen something that made his heart stand still, frozen by the suddenness of faint hope. If he could but lead Wilson on, get him to talk… to delay the end.

"Of course I'd like to know," he grinned. "But you'd better make it good, Wilson. Don't forget about Fifty-Nine Squadron. And don't forget that you've got to get the main force of the British fleet out of their bases before your trick torpedo-laid mine-booms will do any good. Okay, fire away."

"Yes, yes," Wilson murmured, seemingly very pleased by his command of the situation, "you obviously know a little, but not enough. Else you would not talk so foolishly as you do. Listen to me, you swine, and remember my words after I have shot you down like a dog. In just one hour from now the crews of two trawlers loyal to *Der Fuehrer,* and several others of my agents stationed about, will capture Wick in a *Blitzkrieg* so sudden it will be over almost before it has started. The trawlers, the town, the radio station, Fifty-Nine Squadron, the field, and all the pilots and men will be ours. Ours before any word can be sent to the outside!"

The man paused for breath and Combat could almost hear the *thump* his heart made as it fell down into his boots.

"And with Wick in our hands, the rest will be simple!" Thirty-Six shouted, his voice rising like thunder. "My agents will fly the Fifty-Ninth planes here to collect the last of the Formula Q bombs. Those already at Wick will be put aboard trawlers and the trawlers will put to sea to contact a detachment of our fastest submarines, and one or two destroyers. They will steam north, and by the end of two hours Scapa Flow and the Shetland Island naval bases will be completely ringed by our Formula Q mine-booms. When the British fleet comes rushing out tomorrow, the ships will strike our double ring of mine-booms. One by one they will be blown up and sent to the bottom. You saw those boxes placed in that guide torpedo aboard the *Hesse.* Well each of those boxes is enough to doom a ship. The leading ship strikes the chain, and goes down. The parts of the chain are scattered about the surface of the water. They spread out and can hardly be seen. Before the rest of the fleet can turn back, it will be too late. Three-fourths of England's naval force lost in the space of half an hour!"

The spy stopped his speech and panted for breath. His face was livid, and his eyes bulged with wild emotion.

"And a couple of lousy Nazi decoy destroyers are going to bring out the *whole* force at Scapa Flow and Shetland?" Combat snorted. "You must be cracked. True, you may get a couple of British ships that come out to smack off your destroyers, but…."

"Our destroyers?" Wilson boomed at him. "They nor the U-boats will not even be seen! They will stand off miles away and lay the mine-booms by radio control. *They* won't bring out the fleet in full battle force. *Der Fuehrer* will do that. *Herr* Gruber, the greatest leader the world has ever known!"

Bill Combat had no comment to make to that torrent of words. He stared at Colonel Wilson, completely certain that the man had gone mad. The spy returned the look and seemed to read his thoughts. The smile one might see on the face of Satan split the man's lips.

"You think me mad, eh," he said softly. "Ah, no! I tell you the truth, Captain Combat. *Herr* Gruber will cause the British fleet to steam out to its complete doom at dawn. And do you know why? Because right now German troop transports, disguised as cargo boats, are steaming in the Kattegat, and the Skagerrak, and up along the west coast of Norway. By dawn Gruber's troops will have landed and taken possession of strategic strongholds in Norway. Denmark, too, will be in our hands. And what then? When the news of the *Blitzkrieg* invasion of Norway is flashed to England, the whole British navy will be rushed over to try and cut the German navy and troop transports to ribbons. Gruber knows that's just what Churchill will do. He has to send the navy to the rescue or he's shamed, and England is shamed before the whole world. There, *that* is what will bring the fleet into our trap!"

The horrible truth seemed to turn Combat's heart to a lump of stone in his chest. He couldn't speak; he couldn't even think; the room seemed to spin around, and the four walls to press him in. In a dull, abstract sort of way he realized that Colonel Wilson had taken out a gun and was pointing it right straight at his heart.

And then suddenly the air was shattered by a heart chilling, nerve rasping, terrible scream of some one in horrible mental agony!

CHAPTER 17
SPY HELLION

THE SCREAM seemed to release Bill Combat's brain from the life-stifling grasp the horrible significance of Colonel Wilson's words had upon it. He turned his head slightly to see and realized that the tiny hope that had come to him a few minutes ago was bursting into actual reality. Varden Frankle had been listening all the time at the door of his laboratory. He now came rushing out the door, his eyes like balls of fire beneath his shaggy white eyebrows. Behind him Combat caught a glimpse of the sandy-haired Nazi on the floor. The blood-drenched handle of a knife protruded from between his shoulder blades.

Screaming with rage, the aged chemist rushed at Wilson. The master spy was forced to take his gun off Combat to protect himself from the puny blows. He shoved Frankle back. The man stumbled, caught himself, and stood there pouring out the curses of his soul upon Wilson, Gruber, and all Nazism in general. His words left his mouth so fast that they got all tangled up with each other and made little sense. Consternation flooded Wilson's face. He made a few gestures in an effort to quiet and soothe the enraged and betrayed man. He might just as well have tried to hold back the North Sea's tide.

Frankle shouted him down, screamed him down, and cursed him down while Agent Four and the other two Nazis stood there watching Wilson, as though waiting for a sign to go into action. That sign didn't come. It was as though Wilson were momentarily hypnotized by the torrent of abuse that Frankle heaped upon his name, his honor, and everything else about him.

"You have tricked me, you dog of dogs!" Frankle finished up in a hoarse whisper that quickly rose to a scream again. "Well, you shall pay for it with your own filthy life. This time *you shall pay!*"

The chemist spun around and started to race for the laboratory door. The four Nazis leaped after him.

"Catch him!" Wilson bellowed. "He'll blow us all to hell! He'll...."

Colonel Wilson didn't finish. Rather, he finished in a scream of startled terror. The instant the Nazis had leaped after Frankle, Combat had come up off the couch. He had been praying for the moment while the Austrian had screamed his piece. That moment had come, now. Like a striking cobra Combat came up on his feet, grabbed up a chair and swung it with all his might. It caught Agent Four smack on the back of the head and knocked him head over heels into another one of the Nazis. They both went down in a sprawling heap.

The Yank didn't see them spill to the floor, however. No sooner had he bounced the chair off Agent Four than he let go of it. It sailed across the room and smashed into the single light hanging from the ceiling. The light exploded in a splash of flame and then the room was plunged into darkness. Even before the light had gone out, Combat had lunged forward like a star back running interference. He felt his shoulder catch Colonel Wilson, and spin the man like a top. Then, as darkness crashed down, Combat kicked out with one foot, tripped up one of the other Nazis, and got both hands on Frankle.

The chemist started to scream and kick, but Combat slapped a hand over his mouth and pinned him helplessly under his arm. Lugging him around like a sack of meal, the Yank zigzagged through the darkness in the general direction of the door. The room was a bedlam of insane sound, now. Wilson and the other Nazis still conscious were screaming at the tops of their voices. A Luger spat sound and flame, and death thudded into the ceiling above Combat. He ducked impulsively, veered far to the right, then back, and frantically fumbled for the doorknob. He got the door open and lunged through with his burden, just as two more shots plunked into the wood.

Once out in the open he raced to the left, still clinging fast to the kicking and struggling Austrian chemist. Then he veered to the right and ahead. Roots and jutting rocks almost sent him flat a dozen times, but he managed to keep on going—managed to keep on plunging forward blindly in the darkness. His brain raced over at top speed, reliving the journey he had made with his eyes closed to that hidden explosive plant behind the rocky face of the cliff. Twice he was sure he was hopelessly lost, that he would never reach that flat section of plateau where he had smelled the fumes of raw gas and oil. But he had to reach it. He *must* reach it. He knew that Wilson's plane was there, and if he could but get that plane up into the air and take Varden Frankle....

A dark blur suddenly rose up before him, and he almost crashed headlong into it. As a matter of fact he had to fall to his knees and skid along the ground to avoid doing that little thing. But when he was able to make out the shape of that blur his heart looped over in his chest. Lady Luck had indeed guided his stumbling footsteps. He had practically run right into Wilson's plane there on the edge of the night-shadowed plateau landing field.

Staggering to his feet, he raced around the wing to the cockpit and put Frankle down on his feet.

"I *am* English!" he snapped at the man. "Shut up! I'm going to save you from them. I'll get the two of us back into this plane. It's a Hurricane and has plenty of room. Now...."

Frankle screamed curses and broke away.

"I don't want to be saved!" he cried wildly. "I want to die for the terrible thing I have done—what they made me do. They shall die, too. No one will ever know the secret of Formula Q!"

"Come back here, you fool!" Combat yelled, and lunged for the man.

But Frankle sprang out of his reach, whirled and started running away.

"No! No!" his shrill voice trailed back over his shoulder. "I shall avenge myself and my God!"

Shouts and the crack of Lugers, back by the face of the cliff, seemed to punctuate the old man's screams. Combat took two racing steps after him, then groaned and spun back to the Hurricane. He had done his best to save Varden Frankle, and the old man had refused him. There was no more time to waste. Frankle was racing back straight toward his own doom. The thought was heart-breaking, but there was far, far more at stake than the life of one inventive genius. The lives of thousands, perhaps millions of people were at stake. The fate of nations. And he, Bill Combat, had to swing the scales in the right direction.

"Please God, there is time left in which to do it!" he choked out and vaulted into the Hurricane's pit.

HIS HANDS flew like lightning to the ignition, throttle, and button starter. In short seconds he had kicked the powerful engine into life. It roared up in sound, and the sound was punctuated by the sharp crack of a gun close by. He didn't bother to turn his head. He simply kicked off the wheel brakes, snapped on the wing lights and fed high octane gas to the engine. The ship leaped toward a clump of trees. Combat's heart banged up into his throat. He jammed rudder on hard, slithered the ship clear of the tree clump and straightened out.

More trees came hurtling down the beams of his wing lights. Teeth clenched, body braced, he waited until the last split-second and then, hauled the stick all the way back into his belly. The Hurricane quivered, bucked a bit, and then leaped for the clouds, as though taut ropes holding it to the earth had suddenly been slashed through by a knife. The instant he was clear, Combat leveled off and set the nose on a bee-line course for Wick.

In an hour, Wilson had said? In an hour unknown forces would swoop down on Wick and Fifty-Nine and smash them into submission before they even knew what had happened. A Nazi *Blitzkrieg* right on Scotland's shores. In an hour! Had that hour already passed on into the eternity of forgotten time? Combat's whole body shook like a leaf at the thought, and he shot out his free hand for the radio panel. A flip of the power switch and the tubes lighted up. He spun the tuning dial to Fifty-Nine's wave-length, then grabbed the mike off the hook.

"Emergency, Fifty-Nine!" he barked into the mike. "Wick and you are to be attacked by trawler crews and Nazi agents in sector. Arm yourselves for defense. Guard field and hangars. Notify local police and…."

The rest was practically jammed back down Combat's throat as all Scotland seemed suddenly to explode in one terrific hellish roar of sound. Brilliant red spears leaped high into the sky behind him. Concussion waves caught his ship and almost hurled it over and down into a spin. For one horrible second he thought the wings were going to be torn clean off. The compass needle spun around like a top, the altimeter needle went completely haywire as the entire ship vibrated furiously.

Fighting the ship back onto even keel, Combat cast one quick glance back over his shoulder. By then, however, the hellish brilliance of the explosion had faded out considerably. The sky was filled with showers of tiny red and yellow and orange sparks. It was as though the entire celestial universe had been burned out to glowing cinders that were now all falling to earth.

"Your moment of revenge, Varden Frankle," Combat murmured, and turned front. "It was what you wanted, and for your sake, I'm glad. Happy landings, old fellow."

Putting the radio mike to his lips again, Combat started to broadcast his emergency call. But that's all he did, just started… Even as he opened his mouth his eyes fell on the panel. The power signal lights were out. The radio wasn't worth a damn. Varden Frankle had secured his revenge, but its results had reached out across the sky over Scotland and stopped all further attempt by Bill Combat to warn his pals.

Cursing, he hurled the mike away from him, and hunched forward over the stick. The engine was turning up maximum revs and the Hurricane was streaking through the air at close to three hundred miles an hour. But to Combat's agonized brain the ship seemed merely to be limping along with only half the cylinders at work. To the east, dawn was beginning to ooze up over the horizon. The secret of Murdock's farm was gone. It existed no longer—true—but the main British naval forces at Scapa Flow and Shetland were by no means safe.

Wilson had said that there was enough Formula Q bombs and guide torpedoes at Wick to lay a single barrier across both bases—enough to do the job intended. The supplies at Murdock's farm awaiting transport that night were only to make success doubly sure. Perhaps, even now, Wick was in Nazi hands. Perhaps, even now, the Gallant was out to sea and contacting the waiting U-boats and destroyers. Perhaps, even now, guide torpedoes were stealing through the waters about Scapa Flow and Shetland and paying out their long tails of deadly doom for the unsuspecting British fleets.

"Please God, no!" Combat choked and strained his eyes eastward. "Please God, let there be time!"

As though that prayer was to be answered, the light in the east grew brighter. A moment later Combat spotted the thin line that was Wick's shore. Another moment and he found Fifty-Nine's field. He could see that the planes were all lined up on the tarmac, but as he roared closer he could see figures milling about wildly, see the countless flashes as rifles and machine guns spat out their messengers of death. The attack upon Wick had begun! His emergency call had not been received.

And then, suddenly, as the shoreline came tearing up toward him, he saw two trawlers steaming out to sea. They were a good two miles off shore. Their wakes were frothy white and black smoke lay back over the water from their stacks, indicating their engines were being pushed to the limit. For a second, Combat took his eyes off them and glanced down at the fight on the air field. He had no way of telling who was winning. But he did not dare risk the time to slice down and find out. He couldn't strafe the place, either, for fear of hitting his own pals.

But diving down for a look-see, or diving down to strafe, fled his mind as he made his decision. The two trawlers were the important thing. They were well on their way to play their part in Gruber's hellish game, and they had to be stopped at all cost. One lone pursuit airplane against two armed trawlers. The odds were all in favor of the trawlers not being stopped. But Combat didn't give a thought to the odds. He simply stuck his nose down and went streaking after those two boats.

THE TRAWLER crews saw him coming and instantly opened fire. Death sputtered up at him from two different directions. He ignored it completely, concentrated upon the pilot house of the 'Gallant,' and went whanging down in a whirlwind dive, all four of his guns spewing hot nickel-jacketed lead. He saw the figure at the wheel stagger and reel and go toppling over on his face. Combat wasn't sure, but he thought he recognized the ugly face as belonging to the captain.

He didn't bother to take a second look, however. He kicked rudder a bit and trained his guns on two sailors racing forward to take over the wheel. He spilled them flat on the deck in pools of their own blood. Then, kicking the ship up and over, in a wing-screaming half roll, he dropped straight down on the machine gun crew on the after deck, which had been shooting at him constantly. His hot guns wiped them out.

The 'Gallant' was now swinging crazily through the water. Combat quit it for the time being and attacked the second ship. It had two machine gun crews, and they caught him in a deadly cross fire. A spear of white flame raced across his shoulder. A hundred holes appeared in his wings.

Death was slashing up too close and too often. Combat braced himself and whirled the Hurricane around in a dime turn and down. Before the machine gun crews could lower their aim he had put one group completely out of action. Swooping low over the trawler, he put its deck structure between himself and the other machine gun crew. Then, keeping low, he whipped back in a close turn and pumped all of two hundred rounds into the pilot house. The man at the wheel was practically blown through the other side.

That filled the remaining members of the crew with the fear of God. They forgot their gun completely and raced for places of shelter and safety. But there was no place of safety above decks while Bill Combat was in the Hurricane. He mowed down most of them before they could even reach the companionway ladders. There they toppled over like ten pins and fell down on the shoulders of the terror-stricken engine room men who fought to reach the deck and dive over the side.

Then suddenly, as Combat pulled up in a howling zoom, he saw that his work out there over the North Sea was done. Both pilot houses of the trawlers were bullet-riddled shambles, with dead men spilling their blood on the decks. The ships were out of control. The 'Gallant' was heading straight for the second trawler.

Nothing in God's world could stop the sea collision which would occur in a moment.

THE BOW of the 'Gallant' cut into the other trawler like a

knife. Both ships reeled under the terrific impact, and swirling white foam spread out over the water. Then a column of flame shot up out of the engine room of the 'Gallant' and both trawlers were hidden in a great cloud of smoke. Automatically, Combat cut his Hurricane around on wingtip and went racing for distance, just in case the Formula Q bombs were touched off.

They apparently weren't, however. The boiler of the second trawler let go and another fountain of flame leaped for the dawn sky. Then both ships rose up by their bows, as though a giant's hand had reached up from the depths of the North Sea. And then they were gone, taking their cargoes of hellish death out of the world forever.

"Amen to that!" Combat breathed. "I hope…."

He never finished the rest of his sentence, because death came screaming down at him in another form. It was a British Supermarine Spitfire, and all eight of its guns were spewing out ribbons of jetting flame. For a moment Combat was too amazed to move. But the instinctive reaction of a sky veteran saved his life. He went whipping off to the right, then down in a mad powerdive. His subsequent zoom carried him clear of the attacking pilot, who struggled furiously to pull his own Spitfire out of its dive and slam a broadside burst into Combat's ship.

The attacking pilot was a split-second too late, and in that same split-second Combat got a good look at him. As a matter of fact the Yank had to take two good looks before he would believe what his eyes told him. Somehow, in some way, Colonel Wilson had not been caught in that exploding hell at Murdock's farm. There he was in the Spitfire, his face twisted with savage rage, and every frantic effort being used to get his eight guns on Bill Combat.

"So there *was* a spare plane kept at Murdock's?" Combat yelled and swung in toward the other plane. "Just as I thought, eh? No wonder I smelled gas and oil. From that bus you're flying. Pulled under the trees, I guess. Maybe I'm wrong, though. Maybe you do it with mirrors. Well, save a couple of tricks to show the boys in Hell… because that's where you're going, you stinking traitor. And *now!*"

The last word Combat punctuated with a savage four-gun burst of singing death. Wilson saw it coming and came close to tearing his wings off in his wild frenzy to slash out from under and into the clear. But Combat followed through the maneuver foot by foot, and every inch of the way his guns raked that Spitfire from one end to the other. Nothing in the world made by man could have withstood his furious blast of lead, and that Super-marine Spitfire was a thousand light years away from being the exception to prove the rule. It just couldn't last, and it didn't.

The Spitfire staggered through the air as though it had glanced off the top of a brick wall. It fell crazily over on a wing. Then smoke belched out from the engine. Fiery tongues of flame slashed out and licked backward toward the tail. And lastly, the gas tank let go. One second it had been an airplane staggering through the air, and in the next it was nothing but a great shower of flaming embers and smoking human flesh and bones slithering down toward the waters of the North Sea.

"My regards to the devil!" Combat shouted after it, and kicked the nose of his Hurricane around toward the shore.

IN LESS than a minute he was back over Fifty-Nine's field. And in less than half a second after that he realized that there was no hurry. There were a few still bodies lying around on the surface of the field, and a couple of houses in the village of Wick were on fire. But the R.A.F. pilots and mechanics were standing guard over the planes on the tarmac, and local police were herding a group of civilian-clad prisoners away.

Combat cut his throttle and slid around and down to a perfect three point. The Fifty-Nine gang, led by Major Stark, rushed over to him. Blood trickled down from a bullet crease on the C.O.'s cheek, but his smile was a mile wide.

"Your emergency call came through just in time, though something cut you off in the middle of it!" Stark cried, grabbing Combat by the shoulders and shaking happily. "It was close, but we gave them a good beating. R.A.F. can't do anything but fly, huh? The hell we can't. No bunch of Tommies could have done better than this bunch of pilots I've got. But for God's sake, tell me your side of the story!"

"If you'll shut up, I will!" Combat grinned at him.

Then, in as few sentences as possible, he spoke of his experience. No sooner had he finished than the field's radio man came rushing over.

"Major Stark!" the man gasped. "Just got it over the air. The Nazis have invaded Norway. Landed troops at...."

"Go back and get details! We know all that!" Stark barked at him. Then turning to Combat, "Was that Thirty-Six you got?

162

He was really there at Murdock's? Did… did you recognize him this time? Who is he… was he?"

The Yank scowled down at the ground. He was almost tempted to tell Stark, but something Varden Frankle had said flashed through his mind. It was that when two people know a secret, it is not a secret. No, not that Stark would ever tell. Yet, England was still a long way from winning the war. And the people trusted their Government, their Army, their Navy, and their Air Force. Half of victory was keeping public morale high. Now of all times, with Gruber's hordes trying to pour into Norway, was no time to risk the possibility of a General Staff traitor scandal. No, better to let the sudden disappearance of Colonel Wilson remain a puzzle that would be forgotten in the parade of events to come.

"I still don't know who the hell he was," he said quietly. "But he's out of the picture for good, and that's that. How about a night-cap in the mess?"

"Night-cap this time of day?" laughed Stark pointing to the east.

"It may be dawn to you," Combat grinned, "But it's bedtime to me. And tell the desk clerk to call me… say, sometime next month!"

POPULAR HERO PULPS AVAILABLE NOW:

THE SPIDER

❏ #1: The Spider Strikes	$13.95
❏ #2: The Wheel of Death	$13.95
❏ #3: Wings of the Black Death	$13.95
❏ #4: City of Flaming Shadows	$13.95
❏ #5: Empire of Doom!	$13.95
❏ #6: Citadel of Hell	$13.95
❏ #7: The Serpent of Destruction	$13.95
❏ #8: The Mad Horde	$13.95
❏ #9: Satan's Death Blast	$13.95
❏ #10: The Corpse Cargo	$13.95
❏ #11: Prince of the Red Looters	$13.95
❏ #12: Reign of the Silver Terror	$13.95
❏ #13: Builders of the Dark Empire	$13.95
❏ #14: Death's Crimson Juggernaut	$13.95
❏ #15: The Red Death Rain	$13.95
❏ #16: The City Destroyer	$13.95
❏ #17: The Pain Emperor	$13.95
❏ #18: The Flame Master	$13.95
❏ #19: Slaves of the Crime Master	$13.95
❏ #20: Reign of the Death Fiddler	$13.95
❏ #21: Hordes of the Red Butcher	$13.95
❏ #22: Dragon Lord of the Underworld	$13.95
❏ #23: Master of the Death-Madness	$13.95
❏ #24: King of the Red Killers	$13.95
❏ #25: Overlord of the Damned	$13.95
❏ #26: Death Reign of the Vampire King	$13.95
❏ #27: Emperor of the Yellow Death	$13.95
❏ #28: The Mayor of Hell	$13.95
❏ #29: Slaves of the Murder Syndicate	$13.95
❏ #30: Green Globes of Death	$13.95
❏ #31: The Cholera King	$13.95
❏ #32: Slaves of the Dragon	$13.95
❏ #33: Legions of Madness	$12.95
❏ #34: Laboratory of the Damned	$12.95
❏ #35: Satan's Sightless Legion	$12.95
❏ #36: The Coming of the Terror	$12.95
❏ #37: The Devil's Death-Dwarfs	$12.95
❏ #38: City of Dreadful Night	$12.95
❏ #39: Reign of the Snake Men	$12.95
❏ #40: Dictator of the Damned	$12.95
❏ #41: The Mill-Town Massacres	$12.95
❏ #42: Satan's Workshop	$12.95
❏ #43: Scourge of the Yellow Fangs	$12.95

❏ #44: The Devil's Pawnbroker	$12.95
❏ #45: Voyage of the Coffin Ship	$12.95
❏ #46: The Man Who Ruled in Hell	$13.95
❏ #47: Slaves of the Black Monarch	$13.95
❏ #48: Machineguns Over the White House	$13.95
❏ #49: The City That Dared Not Eat	$13.95
❏ #50: Master of the Flaming Horde	$13.95
❏ #51: Satan's Switchboard	$13.95
❏ #52: Legions of the Accursed Light	$13.95
❏ #53: The City of Lost Men	$13.95
❏ #54: The Grey Horde Creeps	$13.95
❏ #55: City of Whispering Death	$13.95
❏ *NEW:* #56: When Thousands Slept in Hell	$13.95

THE WESTERN RAIDER

❏ #1: Guns of the Damned	$13.95
❏ #2: The Hawk Rides Back from Death	$13.95
❏ #3: Gun-Call for the Lost Legion	$13.95
❏ #4: The Law of Silver Trent	$13.95
❏ #5: The Gun-Prayer of Silver Trent	$13.95
❏ #6: Silver Trent Rides Alone	$13.95

G-8 AND HIS BATTLE ACES

❏ #1: The Bat Staffel	$13.95

CAPTAIN SATAN

❏ #1: The Mask of the Damned	$13.95
❏ #2: Parole for the Dead	$13.95
❏ #3: The Dead Man Express	$13.95
❏ #4: A Ghost Rides the Dawn	$13.95
❏ #5: The Ambassador From Hell	$13.95

DR. YEN SIN

❏ #1: Mystery of the Dragon's Shadow	$12.95
❏ #2: Mystery of the Golden Skull	$12.95
❏ #3: Mystery of the Singing Mummies	$12.95